Meow Means Murder – A Norwegian Forest Cat Café Cozy Mystery – Book 2

by

Jinty James

Meow Means Murder – A
Norwegian Forest Cat Café Cozy
Mystery – Book 2

by

Jinty James

DEDICATION

For Annie, my beautiful Norwegian
Forest Cat.

CHAPTER 1

"He's here! He's here!" Zoe raced to the counter, her face alight. Her brown eyes sparkled and her brunette pixie cut looked as if she'd run her fingers through it in excitement.

"Who?" Lauren frowned as she foamed milk for a cappuccino, the hissing of the steam wand punctuating the conversation. In contrast to her cousin, Lauren was one inch shorter, and a little curvy, with hazel eyes. Freckles dusted her nose, and her light brown hair with hints of gold ended at just below her chin.

"The food critic – Todd Fane!"

"Brrt?" Annie, a fluffy Norwegian Forest Cat, trotted to the counter and looked up at Zoe, as if wondering at the commotion.

"Remember the food critic we told you about, Annie?" Lauren leaned over the counter to speak to the cat.

"He's here!" Zoe hopped from one sneaker-clad foot to the other. "Ooh – he's coming in the entrance now!"

"Brrt!" Annie trotted to the *Please Wait to be Seated* sign. The early afternoon sun highlighted the silver in her gray fur.

"Huh." A man in his late thirties with thinning sandy hair and a paunch frowned at the fluffy silver-gray tabby standing in his way. "I guess the description on the website is correct, and not just a gimmick."

"It says the Norwegian Forest Café is a certified cat café," his companion observed. He looked to be in his early twenties, and sported a modern, shaved sides and slicked back on top hairstyle.

"Brrt," Annie seemed to confirm. With a regal air, she swiveled, and led them to a table for two in the middle of the room, her plumy tail waving in the air.

"Annie's showing them to a table." Zoe clutched her cousin's arm.

"Squeeze me any harder and I'll ruin this cappuccino," Lauren said wryly.

"Sorry." Zoe lowered her voice to a stage whisper. "I just can't believe he's here!"

Todd Fane was a popular local food critic, although he usually covered Sacramento eateries. Since Gold Leaf Valley, their small town dating from the 1800s gold rush, was one hour away from the city, Zoe had buzzed as if she'd just downed a triple espresso ever since she'd read on his blog that he'd planned on covering the region.

Lauren was excited as well about the critic, but since they hadn't been sure which day he'd visit – or *if* he'd actually visit their café – she'd been trying to remain calm.

"How do you know what he looks like?"

"He has his photo with his byline," Zoe explained.

"I thought food critics liked to dine incognito," Lauren remarked.

"Maybe he enjoys being recognized. I just hope he gives us a glowing review," Zoe continued. "Like he gave the Gold Leaf Valley Steakhouse last year."

"That would be great." Lauren plated a raspberry swirl cupcake, keeping one eye on Annie and their two VIP customers.

Annie hovered by the VIP table, as if wanting to make sure the food critic didn't need anything. Laminated menus were already on the table, with a sign suggesting customers order at the counter.

The critic and his companion perused the menus.

"I'll take this to table three." Zoe picked up the tray. "You take their order."

"You don't want to?" Lauren eyed her cousin. Zoe had been on tenterhooks for the last week.

"I'm too nervous." Zoe clutched the tray, her knuckles turning white. "What if I drop my notepad or pencil? I don't want him to write about the clumsy waitress."

"Okay." Lauren pulled out her notepad and pen from her apron pocket, which she wore over her usual work outfit of pale blue capris and apricot t-shirt.

When they had an infirm customer, such as the elderly Mrs. Finch, or an imperious one who they knew wouldn't order at the counter, they provided table service.

"Good luck!" Zoe's gaze darted to the VIP table. Annie sauntered back to her pink cat bed on the corner shelf and settled down for a little snooze.

Lauren scanned the room as she approached Todd's table. The other customers hadn't seemed to notice the food critic in their midst. Half the tables were taken, and a low hum of conversation punctuated the space.

"What can I get you?" Lauren smiled at the two men.

Todd, the food critic, looked up from the menu.

"Give me a large mocha and one of Ed's pastries," he commanded. "Whoever Ed is." He smirked and looked at his companion, inviting him to laugh.

Lauren inwardly bristled at the critic's tone but kept her voice pleasant.

"Ed is our very talented pastry chef. But I'm afraid the last pastry was sold half an hour ago." Ed was finishing up in the kitchen. He'd already okayed it with Lauren to leave early that day because he had a dental appointment.

"Oh-kay," Todd spoke slowly. "What do you have left?"

"Raspberry swirl cupcakes, vanilla cupcakes, and cinnamon crumble cupcakes."

"Give me a raspberry swirl," he replied.

"Sure." Lauren scratched out the order on her notepad. "What would you like?" She turned to the younger guy.

He gave her a smile. "I'll have a regular latte and a vanilla cupcake. Thanks." Intelligence shone behind his green eyes and his boyish features looked sympathetic.

"Won't be long." Lauren summoned a quick smile and hurried to the counter.

"Well?" Zoe asked impatiently as Lauren began to make a large mocha.

"Here." Lauren pulled the page off her notepad. "Can you plate the cupcakes?"

"Sure!" Zoe grabbed two white plates and a pair of tongs. "So, what's he like?"

"Rude." Lauren wrinkled her nose.

"Really?" Zoe sounded disappointed.

"The younger guy seems okay."

"I wonder who he is?" Zoe peeked over at their table. "Yeah, he is sort of cute, but too young for me."

"Really?" Now it was Lauren's turn to use that word. "You're only twenty-five."

"And he looks fresh out of college." Zoe sighed. "I don't want to date Methuselah but I also don't want to be a cougar."

"Got it."

Zoe had experienced a dating disaster last month, when her internet date had turned out to be seven years younger than her. Since then, she'd channeled her energies into knitting and had formed a knitting club with three members – four if Annie was included.

"I'd better take this over to them." Lauren gestured to the tray holding two steaming coffees and the sweet treats Zoe had readied.

"I hope they like everything."

"I hope they liked Annie showing them to their table," Lauren replied.

"Who wouldn't?" Zoe looked incredulous.

The Norwegian Forest Cat leading customers to their tables was one of their drawcards, although Lauren always kept an eye on Annie to make sure her hostess duties didn't tire her out.

Lauren headed to the VIP table. "Here we are." She carefully set down the tray and placed the men's orders in front of them. "Let me know if you need anything else."

Todd grunted in acknowledgement, scrutinizing the cupcake from all angles.

"Thanks." The young guy looked appreciatively at his order.

Lauren departed, noticing out of the corner of her eye that Todd had spooned some foam off his mocha and eyed it critically.

"I hope we get a good review," Zoe whispered when Lauren rejoined her at the counter. "Todd wrote in his column that the wagyu at the steakhouse here was out of this world!"

"Have you ever tried wagyu?" Lauren asked curiously.

"No." Zoe shook her head. "It's so expensive! One hundred and sixty dollars for one serving. But everyone raves about wagyu."

"Do they?" Lauren crinkled her brow. "Where?"

"Online." Zoe waved a hand in the air. "And reviews in the newspaper. You know."

Lauren didn't.

"It's supposed to be super tender and delicious. I'd *love* to try it. Maybe we could go one evening."

"You were at the steakhouse last month," Lauren said. "What did you have if it wasn't wagyu?"

"A New York Strip. I couldn't decide between that and the Angus but I decided on the strip. It wasn't bad."

"Let's hope Todd doesn't give us an, *'It wasn't bad',*" Lauren said wryly.

"Look, he's summoning you!" Zoe waved back at the critic.

"I'd better go and see what he wants." Lauren hurried over to the small table, telling herself to be pleasant. She usually kept her patience even with their most difficult customers, but for some reason, the critic's behavior had set her teeth on edge.

Both cupcakes had disappeared, the unbleached paper cases the only evidence. The coffee cups were empty. Hopefully they'd enjoyed it all.

"When can I get one of Ed's pastries?" Todd demanded.

"A few people have told us about them," his companion added.

"Tomorrow morning," Lauren replied. "We open at 9.30 a.m. There should be some ready around ten."

"We'll definitely come back then," Todd said. "We're staying at that dump of a motel a few blocks from here." He scraped back his wooden chair.

Lauren raised her eyebrows at his criticism but didn't say anything.

"I don't think it's that bad," his companion said.

"Here you go." Lauren pulled out the bill from her pocket. "We usually take payment at the counter but if you're in a hurry you can leave the money on the table."

"Huh." Todd looked surprised at being asked to pay. "Sure." He pulled out a black leather wallet and thumbed through a stack of notes. "Keep the change."

"Thanks." Lauren watched them depart. Then she picked up the money and counted it. Sixteen dollars. He'd left a fifty-cent tip.

At least he hadn't tried to argue that he shouldn't pay because he was a food critic. Lauren wasn't sure if he'd expected her to recognize him or not. Maybe she should have sent Zoe over to take their order. Her cousin's excitement at having the man in their café might have put him in a better temper.

"For the tip jar." Lauren put the cash into the register and pressed fifty cents into her cousin's hand. Zoe and Ed shared the tips. Since Lauren made a small profit on top of her wage, it was only fair that her co-workers received the tips as part of their earnings.

Plink. The coin landed on top of others in the glass jar.

"He's coming back tomorrow," Lauren told her cousin.

"Awesome!" Zoe grinned.

Annie briefly looked up from her cat bed, saw that there were no new customers to tend to, sighed, and settled back down on her plush cushion.

The next thirty minutes saw Lauren and Zoe bussing tables and taking payment from customers.

"Brrt!" Annie's ears pricked and she jumped down from her bed, trotting toward the hostess sign.

"Hi, Annie." A girl with long blonde hair swept back with violet barrettes bent down to smile at the cat. "How are you today?"

"Brrp," Annie replied.

Lauren took that to mean, *"I'm good, Cindy. How are you?"*

"Hi, guys." Cindy waved to Lauren and Zoe.

"Hey." Zoe smiled. "How's Gary's Burger Diner today? I'll have to stop by for a burger there soon. Ooh, did Todd Fane visit you? He was here a short while ago."

"Ugh." Cindy made a face.

Annie glanced from Lauren and Zoe at the counter, then back to Cindy, and led the girl to the counter, not to a table.

Lauren gestured toward a table for four in the corner. At three o'clock, there were only a few customers enjoying their orders.

"Why don't we all sit over there for a minute?" she suggested.

"Brrt," Annie agreed, heading toward the table.

"Good idea." Zoe hurried after the cat.

"I stopped by to get a mocha and a cupcake, if you had any left." Cindy eyed the last couple of treats in the glass counter. "But maybe telling you what happened just now would be better."

"Almost better," Lauren said sympathetically. "I'll get you that mocha and a raspberry swirl cupcake in a minute as well."

"That would be great." Cindy's face lit up. "I need cheering up."

"What's happened?" Lauren asked as they joined Zoe and Annie at the table.

"It was awful." Cindy shuddered. "That food critic—"

"Todd—" Zoe interrupted helpfully.

"Yeah." Cindy nodded. "Ugh. What a creep."

"What?" Zoe's eyes widened.

"He came in for a late lunch just now. I didn't know who he was." Cindy's cheeks turned pink. "With waitressing and my college classes, I don't have much time to follow Sacramento food blogs."

"You're studying at the community college, aren't you?" Lauren asked.

"Yes. Anthropology," Cindy replied.

"So what happened today?" Zoe leaned forward.

"He came in after two, and I took his order."

"That must have been after he left here," Zoe remarked.

"He was with a younger guy—"

"Yes, that guy must have been with him here as well," Zoe tapped her cheek. "I wonder who he is."

"You were saying," Lauren prompted Cindy, frowning at her cousin.

"I brought their food out, and he didn't like anything." Cindy shook her head. "You know how good our burgers are—"

"They're the best," Zoe said loyally.

"Brrt," Annie added, having sampled Lauren's take-out order more than once.

"But he said the patty was practically burned, so I took his order back to the kitchen and they made him a new burger. I thought everything was okay after that, but—" she shuddered.

"What happened?" Lauren asked softly.

"His companion had gone to the restroom, and that's when he – Todd – told me that if I wanted my boss to get a good review, I should come out to the parking lot with him!"

"What?" Zoe breathed.

"Wow," Lauren murmured, unable to believe the gall of the man – or perhaps she could, after meeting him today.

"I didn't." Cindy shook her head so fiercely, Lauren wondered if it would fall off. "I would *never* do something like that."

"Of course you wouldn't," Zoe confirmed.

"Brrt!" Annie added.

"And he said if I wasn't "nice" to him, he would write such a bad review, that we'd lose all our customers in a couple of months and I'd be out of a job, along with everyone else."

"No way!" Zoe's mouth fell open.

"What did you do?" Lauren asked.

"Something I regret." Cindy bit her lip. "I picked up his plate and tossed the remains in his lap."

"Yes!" Zoe cheered.

"No," Cindy contradicted. "He stormed out of the restaurant without paying. Then his companion came out of the bathroom and I had to tell him his friend had left. So he left too, and I'm stuck with the bill."

"Did you tell your boss Gary what happened?" Lauren asked.

"Not yet." Cindy twisted her hands. "That place is his baby. How can I tell him that if we get a bad review it's my fault because I wouldn't put out for the food critic?"

"But how could you tell him that you did put out for the food critic for a good review?" Lauren countered gently.

"It's sexual harassment!" Zoe jumped up. "You should report him to the police." Any appeal the food critic had held for Zoe appeared to have vanished.

"Yes." Lauren rose too, then sank down again as she noticed Cindy's doubtful expression.

"I don't want to make a fuss about it," Cindy murmured.

"You're not," Lauren and Zoe said at the same time.

"Brrt!" Annie agreed. She sat next to Cindy and bunted the girl's hand.

Cindy stroked the silver-gray tabby.

"You should still tell Gary, even if you don't go to the police," Lauren gently told the girl. "Just in case this – this *critic* does write a bad review."

"A totally undeserved bad review." Zoe's tone was fierce.

"You're right." Cindy nodded, still stroking Annie. "And I will. But I think I need a mocha and a cupcake first."

"Of course." Lauren glanced toward the counter and the *Please Wait to be Seated* sign, but there weren't any customers standing in line.

"And if you do decide to report him to the police, Lauren knows a guy." Zoe sent a mischievous glance in her cousin's direction.

"Zoe!" Lauren blushed at the thought of Mitch Denman. He was tall, dark, and attractive. And taciturn at times. She'd met him last month when he investigated the death of one of their regular customers. And had barely seen him since.

"You do?" Cindy looked at Lauren.

"He's a detective," Lauren replied, wishing her cheeks would stop flaming.

"And good-looking." Zoe grinned. "And he and Lauren like each other," she added in a sing-song voice.

"Zoe!" Lauren scolded.

"Brrt!" Annie chided Zoe.

"Sorry," Zoe replied, but she didn't look apologetic.

"That's good to know," Cindy replied. "Thanks." She let out a breath. "I feel a lot better now after talking to you about it."

"We'll get your mocha and cupcake," Lauren said.

Annie stayed behind with Cindy, allowing the waitress to continue stroking her.

"I can't believe that food critic," Zoe said with disgust. "To think I was so excited about him reviewing us. And to find out he's nothing but a lech!"

"I know," Lauren agreed. "I just hope he doesn't try anything tomorrow when he comes back for Ed's pastries."

"If he does, we can sic Ed on him!"

The thought of big burly Ed, with monster rolling pins for arms confronting Todd, the food critic, made Lauren smile. Ed made pastry like a dream but valued his privacy, and rarely came out of the kitchen.

"Now you have me kind of hoping that's going to happen tomorrow." Then she sobered. "But that would be bad."

"Would it?" Zoe tilted her head. "He'd deserve it."

"But would Ed?"

"One look at Ed, and Todd would probably run out of the café," Zoe predicted.

That thought cheered Lauren as she made Cindy's mocha. Zoe plated the cupcake and together they took the treats to the table.

"This looks great." Cindy smiled at them as Lauren set down the coffee and cupcake.

"Brrp," Annie said in approval.

"So you're going to tell Gary what happened after you leave here, right?" Zoe encouraged.

Cindy stirred her mocha, then licked thick, creamy cocoa colored foam off her spoon. "Yes," she said. "You're right. He needs to know. I just hope he doesn't fire me."

"Why would he?" Lauren asked. "You must be his best waitress."

"Thanks." Cindy looked pleased at the compliment. "But I need this job."

"Even if he did fire you," Zoe said, "not that he would," she amended hastily, "surely you could get another waitressing gig right away? What about the steakhouse?"

"Maybe." Cindy shrugged. "But Gary's been good to me about fitting in my shifts with school. He's like that with everyone," she added hastily. "Not just me."

"I don't think you've got anything to worry about," Lauren told her.

"If you do, then Gary isn't the guy he seems to be," Zoe added. "And you shouldn't have to work for someone like that."

"You're right." Cindy nodded. "Thanks, guys. I knew coming here was a good decision."

"Brrt," Annie agreed. *Yes.*

Lauren and Zoe left Cindy to finish her mocha and cupcake. Annie stayed with her, her eyes closing in bliss as Cindy stroked the top of her head.

"I hope that *critic* doesn't come back tomorrow for one of Ed's pastries," Zoe muttered. "Because if he does …"

"I'll serve him," Lauren promised, wondering if she actually could. She'd love to turn him away, but would doing so hurt their café's reputation? Whatever her personal feelings toward the critic following Cindy's revelation, she had two employees as well as Annie to think of. She didn't want their café's standing to be savaged in print.

The door opened and a slim, middle-aged woman staggered in, loaded down with a lot of shopping bags.

"Brrp?" Annie asked curiously as she left Cindy's table and trotted toward the newcomer.

"I've been shopping, Annie," the woman with honey-colored hair told her with a smile. "I've bought so many bargains!"

"Brrt," Annie replied, leading her toward a table in the rear.

"That's Kimberly," Zoe murmured to Lauren. "She's married to Wayne."

"Who owns the steakhouse." Lauren nodded. Although she'd only been running the cat café for a few months, she was on friendly terms with the local restaurant owners.

"I wonder what she's bought?" Zoe's eyes sparkled with curiosity. "And where she did all that shopping? Not here in Gold Leaf Valley."

"No," Lauren replied. She enjoyed living in the small town, but she didn't see how it could be possible for someone to buy so much stuff from the local stores.

Annie trotted back to Cindy's table, jumping on a chair and bunting the girl's hand. Cindy smiled and obliged, stroking the Norwegian Forest Cat while finishing her cupcake.

"I'll see if Kimberly's ready to order," Lauren said.

"Good idea," Zoe replied. "She looked ready to drop carrying all those bags."

Lauren headed toward Kimberly's table. Paper and plastic bags of all sizes and colors surrounded her chair.

"Hi, Lauren." Kimberly looked up and smiled at her.

"What can I get you?" Lauren asked.

"That's sweet of you to take my order. I'd love a latte." Kimberly sighed and pushed back her chair, wriggling her red kitten-heeled feet. "I went to the new outlet mall today and walked for miles. You won't believe how many bargains they had there!"

"Where is it?" Lauren asked. Maybe she and Zoe could have a day out there soon.

"Thirty minutes south from here," Kimberly replied. "I meant to go straight home, but I definitely need a coffee first. I had a latte at the mall, but it wasn't nearly as good as one of yours."

"Thanks." A smile tilted Lauren's lips. She prided herself on creating the best beverages and baked goods she could.

"Look what I got!" Kimberly pulled out a jade sweater. "Cashmere. Seventy percent off!"

"Wow." Lauren admired the elegant item.

"Ooh, is that cashmere?" Zoe zoomed to the table. "It's gorgeous!"

"I know, right?" Kimberly beamed. "You should see what else I bought." She started pulling out more sweaters, and a pair of stilettos dotted with pink crystals.

"I wish I could wear those shoes." Zoe sighed.

"Aren't they fabulous? How could I pass these up?" Kimberly waved them in the air. "I'm going to save them for special occasions, like a dinner date with my husband." Her expression dimmed. "If he ever has some free time."

"I guess he must be busy with the steakhouse," Lauren said sympathetically.

"Yeah." Kimberly sighed. "Six nights per week. And then he says he's too tired to go out on his day off."

"Oh." Zoe wrinkled her mouth.

"You don't know the half of it." Kimberly shook her head, her sleek hair brushing against her jaw. "We never seem to do anything as a couple anymore."

"That's a shame," Zoe replied.

"Oh, well." Kimberly shrugged. "Maybe I'll surprise him one night."

A movement at the door caught Lauren's eye and she turned. A man in his early fifties with a burly frame and curly dark hair entered the café.

"Your husband's here," she told Kimberly.

Kimberly brightened.

"Over here, hon!" She waved to her husband.

He waved back and headed toward them.

Annie looked up from Cindy's table, saw that everything was under control, and settled back on her chair.

"I thought I'd stop by for a cappuccino before I start the prep work for tonight," Wayne greeted his wife.

"It looks like we had the same idea." Kimberly laughed.

He frowned as he glanced at the shopping bags surrounding his wife's chair.

"I can't wait to show you my bargains." Kimberly grinned.

"I thought we agreed—"

"Oh, you!" Kimberly wagged a finger at her husband. "It's only a few things, and I actually saved us money by shopping at the outlet mall. I bought you something I think you'll love," she added playfully.

"What can I get you, Wayne?" Lauren asked hastily, feeling like a third wheel.

"A cappuccino with an extra shot would be great, Lauren," Wayne replied.

"Coming right up." Lauren gestured to Zoe to follow her. "I thought we should leave them to it," Lauren murmured to her cousin as they reached the counter.

"Good idea." Zoe scanned the quiet café. "If you don't need me, I guess I'll get started on the dishes."

"Thanks." Lauren gave her a grateful smile. She made the drinks, and carried them to the table. The married couple looked like they were having an intense discussion, although their voices were lowered.

"Sorry to interrupt." Lauren made her voice bright. "Here's your cappuccino, Wayne, and your latte, Kimberly."

"Thanks." Wayne seemed to mask the irritation on his face. "Just what I need."

"I heard Todd Fane the food critic was in the area," Kimberly spoke as she sipped her coffee.

"That's right," Lauren replied neutrally. "He was in here a little earlier."

"How exciting!" Kimberly looked around the room, as if expecting to see the critic. "He gave our restaurant such a good review a while ago."

"I know." Lauren nodded. "Zoe told me."

"You and Zoe should come in sometime and try my wagyu." Wayne set down his cup. "Todd was impressed by it."

"I'll talk to Zoe about it," Lauren replied noncommittally. One hundred and sixty dollars for a piece of steak wasn't in her budget right now, however delicious it might be.

Lauren left the bill on the table and headed back to the counter. Soon it would be time to close up – and then what? After feeding and playing with Annie, her evening was wide open.

She'd probably relax on the couch with her knitting and a TV show.

Maybe Zoe was right – maybe they *should* visit the steakhouse one evening or do something fun after work. They were in their twenties, after all.

"I have to go now, Annie." Cindy appeared at the counter, turning to speak to the silver tabby following her. "I promise I'll come back as soon as I can."

"Brrp." Annie seemed to pout as she looked up at the blonde girl.

"I think you're one of her favorites." Lauren smiled at Cindy.

"She's definitely mine." Cindy beamed at the silver tabby.

"Brrt!"

After Cindy left, Lauren scanned the room. The few customers remaining seemed satisfied with their beverages and baked goods. Only Kimberly and Wayne seemed dissatisfied – but with their discussion, not their orders.

"Dishes are done!" Zoe emerged from the kitchen and joined Lauren at the counter. "Anything happening?"

"Not really." Lauren motioned to Kimberly and Wayne's table. "Apart from their conversation. It looks serious."

"Ooh, Wayne's getting up. Oops." Zoe busied herself, stacking clean china plates. "We don't want him to think we were staring."

"You're right," Lauren replied, pinning a pleasant smile on her face.

"Thanks, girls." Wayne stepped up to the counter, digging out his worn wallet and offering cash. "This is for both our orders."

"Thank you." Lauren rang up the sale and gave him a few coins in change.

"Hope you get a great review from Todd," Wayne said. "The more people who know how good our food is down here, the more business for everyone."

"You're right." Zoe nodded.

After Wayne left, Zoe turned to Lauren. "Do you think we should see if Kimberly would like something else?"

Lauren glanced over at the middle-aged woman's table. She seemed busy checking her purchases.

"Maybe we should give her some time to herself," Lauren said thoughtfully.

"Yeah." Zoe sighed. "I was so tempted to say something about Todd's behavior at Gary's when Wayne mentioned getting a good review from him, but I didn't think I should. It's Cindy's business."

"You're right." Lauren nodded. "It *is* Cindy's business. And I don't think we should do anything to interfere – unless she asks us to."

CHAPTER 2

"Why isn't he here?" Zoe fumed as she scanned the café. It was the next day, and half the tables were already taken that morning.

"It's just past ten o'clock." Lauren checked her practical white plastic watch.

"I don't know if I want Todd to come back," Zoe admitted. "Not after what he tried on with Cindy. But I still want us to get a good review. Does that make sense?" A guilty expression shadowed her face.

"It makes perfect sense," Lauren assured her. Last night, she and Zoe had spoken about Cindy's predicament while watching a crime show, and had finally determined it was up to Cindy to decide what to do, although they would gladly help if asked. She and Zoe had agreed not to mention Cindy's encounter with the food critic to Ed – or anyone else. Not until their friend told them otherwise.

The swinging kitchen door opened and Ed stuck his head through the gap. "The apple Danishes and the pinwheels are ready," he said gruffly. His short auburn hair stuck out in all directions and smudges of flour decorated his black apron.

"Great!" Lauren hurried to the swinging door. "I'll bring them out."

"Hope the critic likes them," Ed said, ducking back into the kitchen.

"I'm sure he will," Lauren replied, the scent of freshly baked fruit and pastry teasing her senses.

Thirty minutes later, there was still no sign of the food critic or his intern, but one-third of Ed's baking had already been snapped up by eager customers.

"This is ridiculous," Zoe grumbled. "If he doesn't come soon we'll be out of pastries again."

"I'll put two of each away for him." Lauren placed two golden apple Danishes and two pinwheel shaped pastries inside a cardboard box, slid it into a brown paper bag, and made a notation in pencil. "There."

"Good idea." Zoe nodded in approval.

An influx of customers snagged their attention, and only one hour later did Lauren realize that Todd still hadn't arrived.

"He should have been here by now," Lauren murmured to herself. She checked her watch. 11.40 a.m.

"Brrt?" Annie jumped down from her bed and trotted over to the counter. *What's wrong?*

"The food critic hasn't returned," Lauren told the Norwegian Forest Cat. "And he seemed keen to try Ed's pastries."

"Brrp." Annie scrunched her eyes closed for a second. "Brrp?"

"Maybe we should check on him." Lauren wondered if that was what Annie had just suggested. She scanned the room. The morning rush had abated and there were only a few tables taken.

"Is he here yet?" Zoe came through the swinging kitchen doors.

"No." Lauren shook her head. "Maybe I should go to the motel and see if he's there." The motel Todd had criticized as a "dump" was the only one in town.

"Yeah!" Zoe's brown eyes sparked. "Maybe you should tell him he's too late to try Ed's pastries!"

"I was thinking I could take the pastries to him," Lauren replied.

"I guess that would work."

"Brrt!"

"I think Annie wants to go with you." Zoe's voice held a trace of amusement.

"Brrt!" Annie seemed to nod.

"Okay." Lauren smiled at the cat. "But you'll have to wear your harness."

"Brr-t." This time it sounded like a grumble.

Annie didn't like wearing her harness when she went out for a walk with Lauren. But Lauren didn't want anything to happen to her, like being startled by a passing car – or worse.

Lauren grabbed the harness from the cottage and fastened it on Annie.

"I think this lavender color really suits you." She stroked Annie's silky soft fur after fastening all the buckles.

"Brrp." *Yes.* Annie nudged Lauren's hand.

They walked out of the café, Lauren waving goodbye to Zoe.

"It's not far to the motel," she told the Norwegian Forest Cat.

"Brrt," Annie replied. She held her silvery gray plumy tail high in the air and gazed at the red maples lining the sidewalk.

"Cat!" A little girl with blonde curls pointed at Annie from her stroller. She waved a chubby hand in the feline's direction.

"Brrt!" Annie replied. *Hello!*

"She's gorgeous," the athletic looking mother remarked to Lauren as they passed each other.

"You can meet her at the cat café down the road," Lauren told her. "And we offer babycinos as well as coffee."

"What's that?" the mother asked.

"It's a little cup of frothed milk with chocolate sprinkles. I think it's an Australian invention." Lauren smiled.

"Cino, cino!" The toddler clapped her hands.

"I'll check it out," the tall woman promised with a grin.

"Cat!" The little girl waved goodbye.

Lauren and Annie reached the end of the main street and turned left.

"The motel is just along here," Lauren told the feline.

Gold Leaf Valley Motel was a Swiss chalet style building and had seen better days, but Lauren thought its fading glamor added a certain type of charm. It was the only accommodation in town, apart from a few small bed and breakfasts, although there was talk of a developer wanting to build a huge motel on the outskirts of Gold Leaf Valley.

Red roses adorned the front garden, along with a lush, green lawn. Although the building could use a coat of paint, the owners maintained the grounds nicely.

"I wonder which room he's in," Lauren said to Annie.

"Brrp?" Annie stopped and looked up at the two-story building.

"We can ask at reception," Lauren told the feline.

Annie led the way to the office at the front of the building. A glowing Vacancy sign hung in the window.

"Hi," Lauren greeted Paul, the owner. Tall and lanky, he made the office appear super small.

"Hi, Lauren." He peered down. "Hello, Annie."

"Brrt," Annie chirped.

"Can you tell me which room Todd Fane is in?" Lauren held up the package containing the pastries. "I have something for him."

"Sure." Paul pressed a couple of buttons on a keyboard and looked at the computer screen. "He's in room seven on the ground floor."

"Thanks."

"Brrt," Annie added.

"Hope he gives you a great review," Paul called as they departed. "You deserve it."

Lauren smiled and waved in reply.

"Here we are," Lauren told Annie thirty seconds later as they stood outside the white painted door with the number seven hanging a little crookedly.

A faint prickling along Lauren's spine gave her pause. Was she nervous about meeting the food critic?

"I'll just hand the pastries to him and we can leave," she told Annie. "We don't even have to step inside the room."

She didn't know whether she was suddenly worried that Todd would expect her to be "nice" to him the same way he'd expected Cindy to be, or if it was something else.

She glanced down at Annie. She stood alert, her ears pricked, and stared intently at the closed door.

"Meow."

Lauren frowned. Annie hardly ever gave a normal meow.

"What is it?" she whispered to the silver tabby.

Annie looked from Lauren to the closed door.

"Meow," she repeated.

Maybe Annie just wasn't keen on meeting the food critic again. Lauren could understand that.

"I'll just knock on the door." She wasn't sure if she spoke to herself or Annie.

Rap, rap, rap.

No reply.

"Should I try again?" Lauren asked the cat.

Annie didn't answer, she just continued to stare at the closed door.

"I'll try once more and then we'll go."

This time, Lauren knocked harder. On the third rap, the door swung inwards a smidgeon.

Lauren met Annie's gaze. The door wasn't locked – or even shut properly?

"Meow!" Annie looked at her with urgent green eyes.

"Mr. Fane?" Lauren called out. What if he was injured? He could have slipped in the shower and hurt himself.

But why was the door unlocked?

"Maybe Paul brought him breakfast and didn't close the door properly behind him," Lauren spoke to Annie. Surely that was it.

Lauren pushed the door inward a little.

"Mr. Fane?"

No answer.

"Maybe we should check he's okay." Lauren bent down to Annie. "Do you think?"

"Meow!"

Maybe Annie's behavior meant the food critic *wasn't* okay.

Lauren took a deep breath and opened the door. She stepped inside the room.

"Mr. Fane, are you – oh!" She dropped the box of pastries, while tightening her grip on Annie's harness with her other hand.

Todd Fane lay sprawled on the carpet, a heavy brass lamp lying beside him.

CHAPTER 3

"Oh no!"

Annie sniffed the carpet around the food critic's body.

Blood seeped from a large wound on his head. His eyes were closed as if he merely slept.

Maybe Todd wasn't dead.

Why hadn't she taken a CPR course? She wasn't sure what to do.

She dug out a small compact from her purse, bent down, and held it under his nose. Was he breathing?

Lauren checked to see if there was a smudge on the mirror, but couldn't see anything, just her reflection.

"What are you doing?"

She whipped her head around. The young guy who had visited the café with Todd yesterday loomed in the doorway.

"We have to call 911!" Lauren grabbed her phone from her bag.

"Is he hurt?" The young guy rushed over to the body. His t-shirt was untucked at the side of his jeans, as if he'd dressed hastily.

"Stay back!" Lauren's tone was sharp. She punched the buttons on her phone.

"Why?"

"I think he might be—" she swallowed "—dead."

The emergency operator came on the line. Lauren gave the room number of the motel and the address, finishing with, "I don't think he's alive."

"Are you sure?" The young guy frowned as she ended the call.

"I don't know how to give CPR, do you?" The coppery tang of blood hit her nostrils, and she flinched.

"No," he admitted.

"I think we should move away from the … crime scene," she told him, leading Annie to the open doorway.

"What happened?" He stared at her.

"I have no idea." She shook her head. "I stopped by to give him some of Ed's pastries." She pointed to the brown paper package on the floor near the food critic's body. "He was already lying on the floor. I thought you and – Todd – Mr. Fane – were visiting the café again this morning."

"Yeah, we were." The young guy nodded. "But then Todd rang me this morning and said something had come up and we'd visit at lunchtime instead."

"Oh."

Annie looked through the open door, sniffing the air. She'd been quiet this whole time.

"Maybe we should step outside," Lauren suggested. Perhaps Annie would feel more comfortable in the fresh air. Lauren knew she would.

"I guess we should introduce ourselves." The young guy held out a hand once they stepped out of the room. "I'm Brandon. I've been working as Todd's intern."

"Lauren." She accepted his brief handshake. "And this is Annie." She indicated the Norwegian Forest Cat.

"Hi, Annie."

"Brrp," Annie said quietly, glancing at Brandon.

"The 911 operator said to stay here and wait for the paramedics," Lauren told him. "And I'll have to tell Paul, I guess."

"Paul?"

"The motel owner." Lauren gestured toward the office.

"I've got the room next to Todd and I heard you knocking on the door. I thought I'd better come and see what was happening."

Lauren nodded in understanding. She took a moment to scrutinize him. His hair looked a little mussed, not as neat as it had appeared yesterday when he and his boss had visited the café. Had Brandon slept late this morning, or was it something else? Like an overnight guest?

The blare of sirens interrupted her thoughts. Paramedics arrived, along with another vehicle.

She bit her lip as a tall man with short dark hair got out of a car. He appeared to be in his early thirties and wore charcoal gray slacks and a white dress shirt. He looked lean yet muscular, as if he worked out regularly.

"Problem?" Brandon asked as she moved aside for the pair of paramedics.

"No." Lauren shook her head, wondering if she fibbed. She took a few steps away from the room, Annie following.

"Lauren." The deep, masculine voice sent a shiver down her spine. So did the straight nose and the mouth that looked like it didn't smile enough.

"Detective." Why did it have to be Mitch Denman investigating the food critic's death – accident – whatever it was?

"What are you doing here?" His dark brown eyes narrowed as he studied her expression.

She repeated what she'd told Brandon.

"I saw her standing over Todd's body," Brandon broke in.

Lauren's eyes widened. Was his tone accusatory?

"But I'm sure she was checking to see if he was breathing," Brandon added.

"That's right." Lauren pulled out her compact. "I held this under his nose." She showed it to Mitch.

Mitch glanced past her into the motel room. Lauren followed his gaze. One of the paramedics shook his head at Mitch as they covered the body.

"It looks like you were too late," Mitch told her.

"I couldn't see a smudge from his breath on the mirror," she admitted.

She'd met the detective last month, when one of her regular customers had been murdered. He was new to town, and after the case he'd stopped in at the café a few times to grab a coffee or one of her cupcakes.

Whenever she saw him, there seemed to be an awareness between them but she wasn't sure if it was all on her side, or if he felt it, too.

Today though, there didn't seem to be a frisson of anything. He exuded pure professionalism.

Brandon explained to Mitch that Todd had been covering the eateries in Gold Leaf Valley for his online column.

"He wanted to expand into the regions surrounding Sacramento," he told Mitch earnestly. "And the newspaper agreed to us staying here instead of going home to Sacramento every night."

"And you accompanied him?" Mitch asked.

"Yeah. It was fun," Brandon replied. "Afterward, we compared notes, and then Todd went back to his room—" he pointed at the open motel room door "—to write a review and post it online. But he was waiting to sample the pastries from Lauren's café—" he gestured to her and Annie "—before he finished writing that review."

"So where were you this morning?" Mitch asked him.

"We were supposed to visit Lauren's café again this morning around ten." Brandon gave her a sidelong look. "But then Todd said he had to do something else this morning, and to meet him at the café at noon."

"Why had his plans changed?" Mitch asked, with an assessing glance at Brandon.

"I have no idea." Brandon shrugged.

"You weren't curious?" Mitch probed.

"Yeah." Brandon fidgeted. "But I've learned not to question Todd when he changes his schedule. He doesn't like being challenged."

"Did you enjoy working for him?" Mitch asked.

"Overall, yes," Brandon replied. "It's a good way to learn the ropes of being a food critic, and he's taught me a lot. Now I look at food in a different way, and I'm more aware of the taste and texture."

"And you said you were going to revisit Lauren's café today?" Mitch waited for his reply.

"Yeah. We went there yesterday and had coffee and cupcakes – which were awesome. But Todd really wanted to taste Ed's pastries and they'd sold out."

"So I told Todd to come by this morning around ten o'clock, so he wouldn't miss out," Lauren interrupted. Instantly she felt guilty for doing so when the full force of Mitch's scrutiny landed on her. "But when he didn't arrive, I wondered if something was wrong, so I came by with some pastries I'd put aside for him," she rushed on. "And when I saw Todd – I dropped them." She pointed to the inside of the motel room, where the brown paper package lay near the heavy brass lamp.

"Annie came with you?" He gestured to the silent feline.

"Yes. I thought she might enjoy the walk," Lauren replied.

Annie looked up at Mitch with interested green eyes, but didn't speak. Was that because Mitch wasn't one of Annie's favorite customers – yet – or because she was overwhelmed by the situation?

"Did anyone see you?" he asked.

Lauren frowned, but told him about her passing conversation with the young mother and toddler, and asking Paul at the motel office for Todd's room number.

"That's all I need for now," Mitch told both of them. "I know where to find Lauren." He turned to Brandon. "But where can I find you? Will you be staying here tonight or going back to Sacramento?"

"I have no idea." Brandon ran a hand through his already slightly mussed hair. "I guess I'll have to call the office and find out what they want me to do." His eyes lit up. "Maybe I'll get to take over Todd's column!" After a second, he grimaced. "I can't believe I just said that."

"It's understandable," Mitch replied.

"So what killed him?" Brandon asked. "The brass lamp?"

"We won't know until we investigate the crime scene," Mitch replied brusquely. "And speaking of which, I need to examine it right now. The room will be cordoned off until further notice, so I hope you don't have any belongings in there." He raised an eyebrow at Brandon.

"Nope." Brandon shook his head.

"Good. If you'll excuse me." Mitch nodded at Lauren, then Brandon, before entering the motel room.

"I guess I'll go back to the café," Lauren said.

"Yeah." Brandon shifted awkwardly. "I'd better call the office and tell them what's happened."

Lauren and Annie headed back to the café, their mood somber. Annie barely glanced around her at the trees, shrubs, and passersby as they returned.

"I'm sorry this happened, Annie," Lauren murmured as they neared the Norwegian Forest Café. The sight of the pale lemon Victorian-style shop attached to her cottage always lifted her heart, and this time was no different, although sadness tempered her reaction. Todd Fane hadn't seemed like a nice man, but had he deserved to die?

"Brrp," Annie said in a subdued tone.

"Do you want to take the rest of the day off?" Lauren asked as they entered the café. "You could play with your toys inside the cottage."

Lauren bent down to unbuckle the harness. Annie stared at her with wide green eyes in a considering manner.

"Brrt," she eventually uttered.

"Okay." Lauren stroked her silky soft gray fur, then stood. "How about some lunch as well?"

"Brrt," Annie replied in a cheerier tone.

They crossed the café. Lauren unlocked the private hall door, walked along the passageway, and into the cottage. She gave Annie a generous helping of chicken in gravy, then blew her a kiss.

"I'll see you when we close this afternoon."

"Brrp," Annie replied around a mouthful of food.

"What happened?" Zoe accosted her as soon as Lauren re-entered the café. "Did you give him the pastries?"

"I'll tell you in the kitchen." Lauren scanned the room. Most of the tables were taken, but no one seemed in need of assistance.

"What did Todd say? Did he love them? You were gone awhile …" Zoe's voice trailed off as her cousin hustled her into the kitchen. "Oh, he didn't love them, did he?"

"Todd Fane is dead." Lauren quickly told her what had happened.

"Oh no!" Zoe clapped a hand over her mouth. "Are you okay?" She looked at Lauren in concern.

"Yes – or I will be." Lauren wrinkled her brow. "I just hope Annie is."

"It's so strange that Annie meowed like that, when you knocked on his motel room door," Zoe mused. "Do you think she must have sensed that he was dead or that something was wrong?"

"She must have." Lauren nodded. "She's hardly ever uttered a regular meow."

"And what about Mitch?" Zoe eyed her cousin knowingly. "What did he look like? Did he mention why he hasn't been here for coffee and cupcakes lately?"

"No." And right now, Lauren didn't want to think about that.

"I'm sure he's still into you," Zoe reassured her. "But he probably needed his mind on the job, asking you and Brandon questions, and then having to look at the – at Todd."

"Probably," Lauren echoed, telling herself not to even think about Mitch right now. She had more pressing issues, such as making sure Annie was okay.

"I bet knitting club on Friday night will cheer up Annie," Zoe said. "You know how she adores Mrs. Finch."

"I do." Lauren allowed herself a smile. Mrs. Finch was one of their regular customers, and one of Annie's favorites. The elderly lady lived nearby and usually visited every day, weather and health permitting.

"Has Mrs. Finch been in today?" Lauren asked.

"No." Zoe shook her head. "If she doesn't visit this afternoon, maybe we should check on her."

"Good idea."

Lauren and Zoe re-entered the café. Luckily, nobody looked like they needed attention.

Nearly all of Ed's pastries had sold. Lauren fleetingly thought of the pastries she'd taken over to the motel, an icky feeling roiling in her stomach, then told herself to stop it.

"What is it?" Zoe laid a comforting hand on her shoulder. "Oh! Hi, Gary." She switched her attention to Cindy's boss standing at the counter.

Lauren had been so preoccupied with her thoughts she hadn't even realized he'd entered.

"Hi, girls." Gary smiled at them. In his early forties, he had pleasant features and short, wavy russet hair. "Where's Annie?" He looked around the café.

"She's having the rest of the day off," Lauren replied. "We visited Todd—"

"Don't mention his name to me." Gary's demeanor changed instantly. He clenched his fists. "I'm not sorry he's dead, after what he tried with Cindy."

"How do you know that?" Lauren stared at him. It wasn't even two hours since she and Annie had been at the motel.

"It's all around town. I guess bad news travels just as fast as good news."

"Huh." Zoe tapped her cheek.

"So Cindy told you what happened?" Lauren confirmed.

"This morning." He nodded. "She came in for her shift, and I could see something was troubling her. When she told me—" a muscle ticked in his jaw "—I was so angry. She should have come to me yesterday when it happened. I would have taken care of that – that – predator."

Lauren and Zoe glanced at each other, their eyebrows raised slightly.

"But you didn't – did you?" Zoe blurted out. Instantly, she looked as if she could take back the question.

"No." He sounded regretful. "One of my kitchen staff didn't show up this morning so I had to do some prep work until I could get someone else to cover for him. I was just about to head over to the motel and give that – *food critic* – a piece of my mind when I heard that someone had killed him."

"Who told you?" Lauren asked.

"I don't know who the source was." He shrugged. "Cindy came into the kitchen and told me a customer had just told her that."

"Wow," Zoe murmured.

"At least Cindy won't have to worry about that creep anymore." He looked at them in satisfaction. "She's a real sweet girl and my best employee. I'm just sorry she didn't feel she could tell me about the incident yesterday."

"I don't think she wanted to upset you," Lauren said gently.

"Knowing what that jerk wanted in exchange for writing a good review is what upsets me." He screwed up his face in disgust. "I just hope this situation never happens again. I'm going to tell all my employees if a customer or critic ever hassles them, to come directly to me and I'll take care of it."

"I bet they'll be glad you've got their back," Zoe said.

"Definitely." But was there a little too much zeal in Gary's voice? Lauren remembered what Cindy had told them yesterday – that his restaurant was his baby.

Gary ordered a latte to go and waved goodbye to them as they left.

"Wow," Zoe murmured after checking no one was likely to overhear them. "Maybe Todd is lucky someone else killed him. Because Gary looked like—"

"I know," Lauren broke in, keeping her voice down. "But we don't know exactly who killed Todd, do we?"

Zoe was silent for a second, then her expression reflected shock. "You don't mean that Gary killed—"

"I didn't say that," Lauren said hastily.

"What *did* you mean?" Mitch asked.

Lauren had been so engrossed in her conversation with Zoe that she hadn't noticed his presence – which might have been a first.

Surprised, she took a step back, accidentally stepping on Zoe's foot.

"Ouch!" Zoe muttered, hopping on one leg.

"Sorry," Lauren apologized.

"What did you mean, Lauren?" Mitch repeated, his gaze zeroing in on her.

"Just what I said," Lauren replied, refusing to feel flustered. "We don't know who killed Todd."

"Do you?" Zoe challenged him.

"Not yet," he admitted tightly. "But it looks like the brass lamp was the murder weapon. We're sending it off for analysis."

"Would you like a coffee, detective?" Zoe gestured to the espresso machine. "Or one of Ed's pastries? There are a few left. And look!" She peered at the glass counter. "Lauren made vanilla cupcakes today."

"Zoe!" Lauren hissed. A few weeks ago she'd learned that Mitch enjoyed her cupcakes, especially vanilla.

"I'm afraid I've got some more questions for Lauren." Mitch glanced over to the empty cat bed. "Where's Annie?"

"Relaxing," Zoe said quickly.

"I thought she might need some time to herself after this – this morning," Lauren told him.

"I see," he replied.

But did he? Mitch had told her when she'd first met him that he

67

didn't have much experience with cats.

"Why are you here?" Lauren blurted out, her face flaming as she realized what she'd said.

"I've got some follow up questions for you." He whipped out his notebook.

Lauren was suddenly conscious of interested glances from her customers.

"We could go outside in the garden," she suggested.

"Great idea!" Zoe grinned at both of them. "I can hold the fort here, no problem."

"I didn't know you had a garden." Mitch frowned.

"It's a small backyard," Lauren told him. "We can access it via the kitchen."

"Lead the way."

Lauren ducked into the kitchen, aware of him following her. What was it about the man that made her feel so self-conscious? There was no sign of

Ed making a last batch of pastries, so he must be on his lunchbreak.

She pushed open the side door and gestured to a small garden. A white picket fence marked the boundary between the café and her cottage. An herb garden to the left contained basil, rosemary, and sage, while a shaggy green lawn dominated the rest of the garden.

"We can talk here," Lauren said breathlessly.

"Okay." He flipped through his notebook, then looked at the grass. "Your lawn needs cutting."

"I know." Lauren felt guilty she hadn't gotten around to doing it. "Zoe and I have been busy with the café." Which was true. The back lawn behind her cottage was almost as bad. "Maybe I can find some time this weekend to take care of it."

"You look after the lawn yourself?" He seemed surprised.

"Yes. There's a lawnmower in the shed." She gestured toward her cottage. "But I'm afraid I don't find yardwork very interesting, although I admire the results afterward."

He nodded, as if he understood. Clearing his throat, he flipped through his notebook.

"Paul, the owner of the motel, said you told him this morning that you had something for Todd Fane."

"That's right. Ed's pastries."

"Nothing else?" He looked at her searchingly.

"No." She furrowed her brow. "I was holding Annie's lead with one hand and the pastries in my other."

Mitch made a notation. "And he said that you didn't tell him that Todd was dead."

"That's right. I was going to, but after I called 911, Brandon and I stood outside the room and spoke for a minute. Then the paramedics arrived, and you …" she trailed off.

"What did you and Brandon talk about?" He looked at her keenly, his dark brown eyes intense.

"We introduced ourselves. He came into the café yesterday with Todd, but I had no idea who he actually was. That was when he told me he was Todd's intern."

"Did he say anything else?"

"I don't think so." Lauren closed her eyes. Maybe it would help her to mentally go over the conversation with Brandon, and it would also shield her from Mitch's assessing gaze. Even with her eyes shut she was aware of the detective's presence.

"No." She slowly opened her eyes. "I don't think so."

"That's all I need for now." He tucked his notebook away.

For some reason she felt disappointed. Why wasn't she glad he didn't have any more questions for her?

She headed toward the kitchen door.

He cleared his throat. "Maybe I could get a coffee to go."

"Of course." She turned back to face him, and smiled.

CHAPTER 4

Lauren and Zoe didn't have a chance to talk until after lunch.

"So what did Mitch want?" Zoe asked when they were both at the counter.

"Not much." Lauren tried to keep her tone casual. "Just if I'd brought anything else for Todd apart from the pastries."

"What a weird question." Zoe scrunched up her nose. "It's not as if you had a brass lamp tucked away in your purse and you hit him over the head with it."

"I know." Lauren furrowed her brow. She hadn't had time to think about Mitch's extra questions until now. Had Paul, the motel owner, said something about her to Mitch? But what? Surely he would have seen her clearly through the open office window.

And why on earth would Paul even think she had anything to do with Todd's death? Todd hadn't given the café a bad review, and hadn't asked anything of her or Zoe in exchange for a good critique. Not like he'd asked Cindy …

"We'll have to talk about this later," Zoe said as a couple of customers came to the counter, ready to pay.

Lauren nodded, already giving change to the first person in line.

Half an hour later, an elderly lady shuffled through the front door, her cane tapping along the wooden floorboards.

"Mrs. Finch!" Lauren hurried to greet her. "Zoe and I were going to check on you after work today if you hadn't dropped by."

"I'm fine, Lauren." Mrs. Finch's wrinkled face wreathed into a smile, highlighting a spot of orange rouge on each cheek. Her pink lipstick was a little smudged, and her gray hair was twisted in a slightly untidy bun, but otherwise she looked well.

"Let me show you to a table." Lauren walked slowly, not wanting to rush her.

"Where's Annie?" Mrs. Finch inquired.

"She's having a rest today," Lauren replied. "I'll tell you about it in a minute."

Lauren scanned the room, her gaze alighting on a small table that wasn't too far from the entrance. Perfect. She thought Annie would have chosen the same table.

She waited until Mrs. Finch was seated, then sank down into the chair opposite.

"Annie is alright, isn't she?" Mrs. Finch asked anxiously.

"She's fine," Lauren replied. "But she – we – had a disturbing morning." She quickly told Mrs. Finch about their trip to the motel and what they had discovered. Mitch hadn't warned her not to tell anyone. And she wanted to put the senior's mind at rest about Annie.

"Oh, my." Mrs. Finch put a trembling hand to her mouth. "That's terrible, Lauren."

"Yes, it is," Lauren replied soberly. She hadn't told Mrs. Finch about Cindy's experience with the food critic, though.

"How are you holding up, dear?" Mrs. Finch asked.

"I'll be okay." Lauren gave her a reassuring smile. She didn't want the elderly lady to worry. "I gave Annie lunch when we got back from the motel, and gave her the rest of the day off to just relax and play with her toys."

"You will give her a pat from me, won't you?"

"Of course. And we'll be coming to your house on Friday night for knitting club. Annie too."

"That will be lovely." Mrs. Finch smiled.

Lauren took the senior's order for a pot of tea and a vanilla cupcake – one of the last cakes left in the glass counter.

"I'm glad Mrs. Finch is here," Zoe murmured as she looked up from the cappuccino she was making.

"I know." Lauren plated the cupcake and grabbed a small white teapot. "I worry when she doesn't come in."

One of their most regular customers, Mrs. Finch enjoyed chatting with Lauren and Zoe, but Lauren thought Annie was the big drawcard. The feline usually sat with her the whole time she was in the café.

"I told her we're on for knitting club this week," Lauren informed her cousin.

"Good." Zoe wiped the milk wand with a damp cloth. "But I think I'm tired of knitting."

"What?" Lauren spilled a little of the loose-leaf tea. "You knitted Annie two blankets."

"I know." Zoe nodded as she sprinkled chocolate powder on top of the cappuccino. "And the second blanket looked pretty awesome. That's the problem. Now I've mastered garter stitch, I've gotten a bit bored with it."

"But there are so many other stitches to learn," Lauren argued. She still struggled with knitting her scarf in garter – at this rate, it wouldn't be ready until winter next year, but she was determined to finish it.

"True." Zoe picked up the tray with the steaming beverage. "But I was thinking … maybe I should try crochet instead."

"Crochet?" Lauren mouthed after her cousin. Zoe threaded her way through the tables to a sophisticated woman studying a laptop screen.

Lauren took Mrs. Finch's order over to her.

"Thank you, dear." Mrs. Finch smiled at her. "I do so love your tea, Lauren. Somehow it tastes better than when I make it at home."

"Thanks." Lauren smiled. "How's your coffee machine?" A few weeks ago, Mrs. Finch had begun using a pod machine.

"I think I need some more capsules." She frowned. "I looked in the grocery store but I wasn't sure which ones to buy. There were so many to choose from."

"I'm sure Zoe and I can help you." Zoe had bought the first box of pods for Mrs. Finch, and she and Lauren had set up the machine for the elderly lady.

"That would be wonderful." Mrs. Finch picked up her teacup with a wobbly hand. "Perhaps you could write me a list of which ones I should get when you come over for knitting club."

"Will do," Lauren promised with a smile.

When she returned to the counter, Zoe was already there.

"What did Mrs. Finch say?" she asked.

"She needs some more coffee capsules."

"We can buy her some on the way to knitting club," Zoe said.

"Good idea. And you can tell her all about your crochet plans." Lauren paused. "Do you know what you want to make?"

"I'll think I'll make a scarf." Zoe giggled. "Not like yours, though. I saw this amazing looking yarn in the handmade shop the other day. It's multi-colored. And there was a ball that had pink, orange, jade, and turquoise colors. I can just imagine wearing a scarf like that when it's cold!"

Lauren could already see her cousin wrapped up in one like that. Now her work-in-progress red scarf sounded dull in comparison.

"So, are you going to start it tomorrow?"

"Yep. Maybe Mrs. Finch knows how to crochet as well as knit! Otherwise I can watch some videos online – and find a pattern, of course."

"Sounds like a plan." Lauren smiled. Her cousin had held a variety of temp jobs over the years, until she'd joined Lauren in Gold Leaf Valley. Maybe exploring hobbies was now Zoe's way of trying new things.

Lauren and Zoe kept an eye on Mrs. Finch, Lauren hurrying over with the bill when it looked like she had finished. She didn't want to burden Mrs. Finch with expecting her to walk over to the counter to pay.

"I can take your payment," Lauren said.

"Thank you, dear." Mrs. Finch pressed some money into her hand.

"Zoe said we'll bring some coffee pods over to you Friday night."

"You two do look after me." Mrs. Finch patted Lauren's hand. "And Annie, of course."

"You two can catch up at knitting club."

"We definitely will," Mrs. Finch said in all seriousness.

Lauren escorted her to the door. Mrs. Finch waved away her offer of walking her home.

"I'll be fine, Lauren. I only live around the block."

Lauren and Zoe watched her walk along the street, until she was out of sight.

"She seems okay," Zoe remarked.

"Yes." Lauren gave a relieved smile. "I just hope I'm as independent at that age."

"Me, too." Zoe nodded.

The rest of the afternoon rushed by, giving Lauren no time at all to think about what had occurred that morning. Which was probably for the best.

CHAPTER 5

The following day, they had just opened when the mother from yesterday arrived, pushing her blonde toddler in the stroller.

"Hi!" Lauren greeted her.

"Brrt!" Annie trotted over to the *Please Wait to be Seated* sign.

"Cat!" The little girl waved her hands and feet in the air. One chubby hand clutched a small brown teddy bear.

"Molly wouldn't stop talking about you two." She pushed a strand of blonde hair away from her face. "The first thing she said this morning was 'cat'."

"Annie will choose a table for you." Lauren gestured to the feline.

"Really?" The thirty-something mother's face lit up. "That's certainly something different."

"Brrt!" Annie agreed. She led them to a four-seater table in a secluded corner.

"Maybe I should go over and take their order," Lauren murmured to Zoe.

"Good idea. They're our only customers, but she mightn't want to leave her little girl on her own, even if Annie's there." Zoe gave an amused glance at the trio. Annie had jumped up on one of the chairs and was staring at the toddler in fascination.

Lauren and Zoe both ended up going over.

"What can we get you?" Lauren asked with a smile. "I'm Lauren, and this is my cousin Zoe."

"I'm Claire," the mother replied.

"Cino! Cino!" the toddler chanted.

"Our babycinos are awesome," Zoe told the little girl. "They have chocolate sprinkles on them and come with a marshmallow."

"Yeah!" Molly beamed, hugging her teddy bear.

"I'd love a double shot latte." Claire pointed to the laminated menu. "What sort of pastries and cakes do you have? I can go over and take a look." She began to rise.

"Our cakes and pastries are made fresh every day," Zoe replied. "Today, Ed is making apricot Danish."

"And I've baked lemon poppy seed cupcakes, cinnamon coffee cake, and my new triple chocolate cupcakes," Lauren added.

"Triple chocolate …" Claire's voice trailed off as a dreamy look crossed her face.

"I use a chocolate cake batter, then add Belgian dark chocolate chips as well as white ones. Each cupcake has a generous swirl of dark chocolate ganache on top," Lauren informed her.

"I have got to try that," Claire murmured.

"Choccy, choccy," the toddler sang.

"You can have a little bit of mine," Claire told her daughter.

"Won't be long," Lauren promised. She hesitated. Annie had been quiet during the exchange. "Are you okay with Annie sitting with you?" She gestured to the silver-gray tabby. So far, they didn't have many small children as customers.

"Mind?" Claire grinned. "She's the main reason we came."

"Awesome." Zoe beamed.

"Cat, cat." The toddler held her hand out to Annie.

Annie sniffed it, then bunted the girl's palm.

"I think Annie would like it if your daughter patted her," Lauren said.

"Gently, darling," Claire told the toddler. "Fairy pats."

Molly nodded, giving Annie feather light strokes on her shoulder.

"Brrt," Annie chirped.

"That means she likes it," Zoe told them.

"This place is just wonderful." Claire gazed around at the pale lemon walls, and the pine tables and chairs. "I can't believe I haven't been here before."

"We've only been open for a few months as a cat café," Lauren told her. "Before that, my grandmother ran it as a regular café."

"We've just moved here a couple of months ago from L.A. We wanted to get out of the city and live somewhere quieter," Claire remarked.

"It's definitely quieter around here," Zoe informed her cheerily.

If you don't count two murders in two months.

Lauren and Zoe hurried to the counter. "I'll make the latte and babycino if you plate the cupcake," Lauren suggested.

"Sure thing, boss." Zoe grinned.

While they worked, a couple more customers arrived. Annie came over to greet them and lead them to their tables, then trotted back to the toddler and her mom.

"It's usually busier than this in the morning," Zoe muttered.

"I know." Lauren shook a generous helping of chocolate powder on the not-too-hot milk foam that was the basis of the babycino, then added a marshmallow on the side. She served it in an espresso cup – just the right size for children.

"I'll take these over." Lauren grabbed the tray and walked over to Claire.

"Let me know if you'd like anything else." Lauren carefully placed the babycino in front of the toddler. "The foam isn't too hot."

"That looks wonderful." Claire looked admiringly at the silky white foam, the lavish serve of chocolate powder, and the pink marshmallow.

"Cino, cino!" The little girl clapped her hands in delight.

Annie looked inquiringly at the babycino.

"The chocolate powder isn't good for you," Lauren told the cat. "And I don't think the marshmallow would be, either."

"Brrp." Annie seemed to understand, although she sounded disappointed.

"And mine looks wonderful, too." Claire plunged her fork into the triple chocolate cupcake and closed her eyes as she tasted the combination of ganache and cake. "That's incredible." She blinked as she slowly opened her eyes.

"Thanks." Satisfaction filled Lauren. She loved it when customers appreciated her baking.

"I must buy another triple chocolate to take home with me."

"I'll take care of that right now." Lauren grinned as she hurried back to the counter.

"Another satisfied customer – make that two customers?" Zoe asked hopefully as she studied the trio at the table.

"Yes." Lauren busied herself with the to-go order. "Claire loves the cupcake."

"Who wouldn't?"

"My waistline." Lauren looked ruefully at the waistband of her blue capris.

"Men like a bit of curve. I'm sure of it." Zoe glanced down at her straight-waisted figure. "Sometimes I wish I looked like you."

"And sometimes I wish I looked like you." Lauren shook her head in wonder.

"Well, from now on, we're going to believe we're perfect just the way we are," Zoe declared.

"You're right." Lauren nodded. She'd tried diets in the past and had been miserable on them. If tasting her sweet treats was a crime, then so be it. If she couldn't indulge in a cupcake when she needed – wanted – *needed* one, then her curvy figure was the price she would pay.

Annie stayed with Claire and Molly until they left, the happy girl waving goodbye to Annie, alternately chanting, "cat" and "cino" all the way to the door.

"Are you open every day?" Claire asked hopefully.

"We're closed on Sundays and Mondays," Lauren told her. "And Saturday afternoons."

"We'll definitely visit again next week," their new customer promised.

"Brrt!" Annie sounded approving.

The rest of the morning passed by in a blur. After a slow start, they had plenty of customers, resulting in the triple chocolate cupcakes selling out by lunchtime.

Zoe looked mournfully at the empty glass case. "I was going to have one for lunch."

"Me too." Lauren sighed. "I didn't expect them to be such a big hit."

"Promise you'll make more tomorrow."

"I will."

"They've even outsold Ed's apricot Danish." Zoe cheered up.

"That might be a first." Lauren smiled. Sometimes she thought Ed's pastries were just a little more popular than her cupcakes. And after having sampled plenty of them, she could understand why.

Lauren and Zoe barely had time for a lunch break. The room was packed, all the customers talking about the food critic's murder.

But Lauren didn't see Brandon come in. She didn't know if he'd already returned to Sacramento or was still in town. Would the newspaper let him take over Todd's column since he was an intern?

Lauren had no idea if her café would still be reviewed. She just hoped that Todd hadn't had time to post a bad review about his experience at Gary's. When she had a chance tonight, she could search online and see if anything came up for Gary's restaurant.

They were just about to close up at five that afternoon, when Claire rushed back in, Molly sobbing in the stroller.

"What's wrong?" Lauren hurried over.

"Want Bear," the little girl wailed. Her face was wet with tears.

"We've lost her teddy bear," her mother said. Her face was flushed and she looked like she'd run all the way to the café pushing the stroller. "Molly says he came with her this morning but I can't remember when I saw him last. It could have been here or it could have been back home later today. But I've searched the house and I can't find him."

"Bear," Molly sobbed, kicking her feet.

Lauren looked around the café. All the customers had departed and Zoe was stacking chairs on the tables.

She called her cousin over and explained the situation.

"I haven't noticed anything out of the ordinary." Zoe crinkled her brow. "What does the bear look like?"

"He's a small brown bear. That's his name actually." Claire gave them a tired smile. "Bear. Molly takes him everywhere."

A thought struck Lauren. Last month, Hans, one of their regulars, had left his spectacles behind, and Annie had been the one to find them.

"Annie," she called.

The Norwegian Forest Cat was already making her way over to them, her expression curious. Was she wondering why Molly was crying?

"Have you seen Molly's teddy bear? It's small and brown. And furry."

"Brrp." Annie tilted her head to one side, as if considering the question.

"Bear," the toddler sobbed.

Annie turned and headed toward her cat bed on the shelf. But instead of jumping up, she nosed around underneath the shelf, her plumy tail waving back and forth as she searched a corner.

"Brrt." The sound was muffled as she turned around and trotted toward

Molly with the teddy bear dangling from her mouth.

"Bear!" Molly hugged the stuffed toy to her, her tears drying up. "Bear!"

"Thank goodness." Claire breathed a sigh of relief. "Thank you, Annie."

"Brrt," Annie replied, looking pleased at the praise.

"Fank you, Annie," Molly said, reaching out to gently pat the cat, tightly clutching the teddy in her other hand.

After promising to come in again next week, Claire and her daughter left, Molly laughing and hugging her toy.

"Phew!" Zoe dramatically mopped her brow. "Crisis averted."

"Thanks to Annie." Lauren smiled at the cat.

"Brrt," Annie agreed, her mouth tilting upwards, as if she smiled.

"I was going to sweep the floor boards after I finished stacking the chairs," Zoe said. "But I'm glad Annie found Bear."

"Me too."

Lauren and Zoe finished closing up.

"If I hurry, I might be able to catch the handmade shop and buy that crochet yarn, and some coffee pods at the grocery store." Zoe checked her watch.

"Okay." Lauren smiled.

After a quick dinner, Lauren, Annie, and Zoe set out to Mrs. Finch's house.

"I can't wait to show her my yarn." Zoe dangled the paper bag that contained her new purchase. "And the espresso capsules I bought for her."

"I think she'll like both." Lauren had seen the balls of yarn and they looked exciting and colorful.

"Brrp," Annie agreed, wearing her harness. She walked beside Lauren and seemed to enjoy the admiring glances a couple of passersby gave her. The memory of walking in her harness to the motel and discovering the food critic's body with Lauren did not seem to bother her today.

They turned into Mrs. Finch's street. Orange and yellow poppies, almost the same color of the sun low in the sky, dotted her neat front garden.

Zoe knocked on the door.

"Hello, girls." Mrs. Finch looked pleased to see them. She wore a pastel blue pantsuit and leaned on her cane.

"Hi, Mrs. Finch," Lauren greeted her.

"Come in, come in." She ushered them down the lilac painted hall and into the living room.

"Oh, Annie, it's so lovely to see you." She beamed at the Norwegian Forest Cat.

"Brrp," Annie said, brushing against Mrs. Finch's leg.

Lauren unbuckled the harness. This wasn't the first time Annie had been to knitting club and Mrs. Finch delighted in seeing the cat being able to move around freely.

"How is your scarf coming along, Lauren?" Mrs. Finch asked, settling into a fawn armchair. The carpet was beige, and the pulled back drapes were of a similar hue.

"I'm not sure I'll ever finish it." Lauren sighed as she sank down onto the sofa.

"I'm going to make a scarf, too." Zoe grinned, waving her paper bag. "But I've decided to learn crochet, Mrs. Finch!"

"Crochet?" She looked surprised. "But your knitting was coming along so well."

"It was." Zoe nodded. "But now I feel like I need a new challenge – so it's crochet for now. And look!" She pulled multi-colored yarn out of the bag, like a magician producing a rabbit out a hat. "Isn't it fun?"

"Why, I haven't seen anything like this before." Mrs. Finch fingered the worsted weight strands, one bold primary color slipping into the next. "I can just see you in a scarf made from this." She looked up at Zoe.

"Do you know how to crochet, Mrs. Finch?" Zoe asked hopefully.

"Yes, I do. But it's a been a while – a very long while."

"Then you'll be able to teach me the basics!" Zoe pulled out a pattern from the paper bag. "I picked this up at the shop, and a hook. So now I can get started tonight!" She plopped down on the sofa and looked at Mrs. Finch expectantly.

"Zoe also bought you some coffee pods," Lauren said.

"Oops! That's right." Zoe jumped up and rummaged in her large red purse. "Here you are." She held out a cardboard box to Mrs. Finch.

"Why, thank you, dear." Mrs. Finch peered through her spectacles at the label. "These look different to the first ones you got for me."

"They are," Lauren said. "We thought you might like a change."

"Brrt," Annie agreed. She sat next to Lauren on the sofa.

"That's so thoughtful of you, dears." Mrs. Finch smiled at them. "We could try them tonight."

"Great idea!" Zoe beamed.

Lauren started on her knitting, while Zoe perched on Mrs. Finch's armchair, learning crochet. Annie wandered over to them, and patted the dangling jade yarn.

"Annie wants to crochet, too." Zoe giggled.

Lauren left her cousin and Mrs. Finch to the intricacies of crochet, finding the motion of wrapping her red wool around the knitting needles soothing. She let her thoughts drift.

Who could have murdered Todd? Why? When they returned home, she'd have to get Zoe to check online and see if Todd had posted a review for Gary's eatery before his death. She hoped if he had, it wasn't a bad critique.

Who knew Todd was staying at the motel? It was the only place in town, apart from a few private bed-and-breakfasts, so it would be easy to assume that's where he and Brandon would stay.

Brandon. The intern definitely knew which room was Todd's – he'd been occupying the room next door.

But why would Brandon kill Todd? He'd admitted to Lauren and Mitch that he couldn't assume he'd get the opportunity to take over Todd's column because of his inexperience.

And if Brandon was innocent, then why hadn't he heard the killer next door with Todd? He'd claimed he'd heard Lauren knocking at Todd's door when she'd found his body, so why hadn't he heard the murderer?

"Lauren?" Zoe's bubbly voice broke into her thoughts.

"Hmm?" Lauren blinked and looked over to her cousin.

"Look! I've just learned chain stitch!" Zoe waved a dangling line of yarn. "And now I'm going to learn my second crochet stitch!"

"How is your scarf coming along, Lauren?" Mrs. Finch asked.

Lauren held up her work in progress. Tonight, only a couple of sneaky holes had managed to appear in her garter stitch.

"That looks lovely, dear." Mrs. Finch smiled at her. "I'm sure you'll finish it by winter."

"Do you think so?" Lauren asked hopefully. "Because I've been thinking it mightn't be ready until the winter after next!"

The three of them laughed. Annie looked amused, her green eyes sparkling.

"Why don't I make us all a coffee?" Zoe hopped up. "We could try your new capsules, Mrs. Finch."

"That would be delightful. And then you can tell me more about this murder."

Lauren and Zoe exchanged a glance.

"What would you like to know?" Lauren ventured.

"Do you girls know who did it?"

"Of course not!" Zoe sounded shocked.

"Brrp," Annie added. *No.*

"Let's make that coffee." Lauren rose.

Lauren and Zoe hurried to the kitchen.

"Do you really think we should discuss the case with Mrs. Finch?" Zoe asked as she turned on the machine.

"I'm not sure. There's no way Mrs. Finch could be a suspect this time."

"I can't believe we ever thought of her as a person of interest last time," Zoe remarked.

"I know." Lauren smiled ruefully. "I don't see what else we can tell her," Lauren said as they made three coffees, the machine growling loudly each time it extracted the espresso from the pod.

She opened a cupboard and got out a small bowl, perfect for Annie's water. Mrs. Finch had given her permission weeks ago to use her china for Annie's use.

"I don't want the little darling to feel left out when we have a drink but she doesn't," the elderly lady had explained her reasoning one evening.

"Maybe Mrs. Finch knows something!" Zoe turned off the machine, and added warmed milk to each cup, since there wasn't a milk frother available. "Maybe she's heard something and wants to tell us!"

"Like what?"

"That's what we're going to find out!" Zoe grinned, picking up two of the floral mugs.

Lauren carried in Annie's bowl of water, then returned to the kitchen for the third coffee.

"It smells lovely, Zoe." Mrs. Finch picked up her cup, her hands wobbling slightly. Zoe had recently converted her to coffee, after showing her how to use the machine, which had been a gift from her son in New Mexico.

"Thanks." Zoe looked pleased.

"Brrt." Annie lapped at her bowl, her little pink tongue making darting motions in the water.

"Mm." Lauren sipped her coffee. "Good choice, Zoe."

"I went for medium roast, with spicy notes of chocolate." Zoe grinned.

"I think I like this pod slightly better than the first variety," Mrs. Finch admitted.

"I'll buy you this one again next time," Zoe promised.

After they sipped their coffees, Mrs. Finch cleared her throat.

"Do you girls know anything more about the murder?" she tried again.

"No." Lauren shook her head and looked at Zoe.

"No," Zoe replied after a moment.

Lauren let out a breath she hadn't known she was holding. She was glad

Zoe hadn't uttered a word about Cindy's run-in with the food critic before his death.

"Well, that's too bad." Mrs. Finch looked disappointed. "I was sure you girls would be up to date with it all."

"I believe the police are investigating it thoroughly," Lauren replied.

"Very thoroughly." Zoe winked at Mrs. Finch. "Mitch – Detective Denman – came into the café to ask Lauren some more questions."

"What did he say?" Mrs. Finch asked.

"He wanted to know if I'd brought anything else to Todd's motel room besides Ed's pastries," Lauren said.

"Why would he ask that?" Mrs. Finch frowned.

"I have no idea." Lauren shrugged. "Apparently Paul, the owner of the motel, told him I stopped by the office to find out Todd's room number."

"I bet Mitch just wanted to see you again." Zoe giggled. "So he came by the café to ask you that question."

"There were a few others," Lauren admitted.

"Like what, dear?" Mrs. Finch leaned forward.

"He asked if Brandon said anything else to me, stuff like that."

"And did he?" Mrs. Finch asked.

"No." Lauren shook her head.

"Brrp." *That's right.*

Annie jumped up on the sofa and bunted Lauren's hand.

Lauren stroked the Norwegian Forest Cat's silky fur, the motion soothing her.

"So who do you think did it?" Mrs. Finch asked.

"I have no idea," Lauren replied.

"Me, neither." Zoe sighed. "There's no way it could be Gary."

"Gary?" the senior queried.

"He runs Gary's Burger Diner and makes amazing burgers." Lauren shot

Zoe a warning look. She wanted to keep Cindy's confidence.

Zoe looked sheepish.

"Why would he be guilty?" Mrs. Finch asked.

"Todd tried their food," Zoe said with a forced laugh. "Apparently he didn't like it much."

"I've never been there," Mrs. Finch admitted. "But some of my friends at the senior center said their grandchildren love the burgers there."

"We like them," Lauren said. "So does Annie."

All three of them gave the cat a fond look.

"I thought you girls might have found out whodunit," Mrs. Finch continued. "Like you did last time."

"I don't know what Mi – Detective Denman would think about that," Lauren replied.

"We don't want to do anything to spoil their budding romance." Zoe winked at Mrs. Finch.

"Zoe!" Lauren blushed.

"But you didn't interfere last time, did you?" Mrs. Finch asked. "You just picked up tidbits here and there."

"I suppose so," Lauren said slowly.

"Brrt!" Annie added.

Lauren stroked the Norwegian Forest Cat's fur. If it hadn't been for Annie last month helping them catch a killer, she and Zoe mightn't be here right now.

"I don't know if there's anything we can do this time." Zoe sipped her coffee. "We're not suspects—"

"As far as we know," Lauren interrupted. Why had Paul said something to Mitch yesterday? She hadn't done anything shady by bring the food critic Ed's pastries – or had Paul thought she had?

"Oh." Mrs. Finch's expression fell. "Well, I hope the police catch the killer, even if you girls aren't helping them."

"Brrt," Annie agreed.

The rest of the evening passed in knitting, crocheting, and coffee drinking. By 9.30pm, Zoe had created three rows of her scarf in double crochet.

"Look!" She held it out to Lauren. The pink, orange, red, and jade colors, in a pattern of strands and spaces, looked fun and exciting. "No holes, either." She grinned. "And if I do get one, it will just look like part of the pattern!"

"Maybe we should have started off with crochet instead of knitting." Lauren stared gloomily at her scarf. She'd done some more rows tonight, and somehow *another* hole had crept in.

"Once you've finished your scarf, you can try crochet next, too." Zoe patted her shoulder encouragingly.

"I might." Lauren put away her knitting and yawned. "We'd better get going, Mrs. Finch. We have to get up at six tomorrow."

"All right, dears." The senior seemed a little disappointed that knitting and crochet club was over.

"You're right – you girls need your sleep if you're opening the café tomorrow."

She walked them to the front door, Annie brushing against her legs before they left.

"See you soon, Mrs. Finch!" Zoe waved goodbye to her.

"I think I like crochet better than knitting!" Zoe skipped down the path and out onto the street.

"I'm glad you had fun." Lauren smiled as she held Annie's harness. The feline trotted along in the dark, sniffing an occasional plant along the way. The gloom was illuminated by glowing yellow lamp posts.

"Now all we have to do before we go to bed is see if there's a new online review for Gary's Burger Diner."

CHAPTER 6

"I can't see anything." Zoe peered at the screen again. "No new review for Gary's burgers."

"That's good, isn't it?" Lauren looked over her cousin's shoulder.

"It could be." Zoe sounded doubtful. "But this webpage doesn't even mention Todd's death."

It was true. A photo of Todd still appeared at the top of the site, but so far there hadn't been any new reviews posted about Gold Leaf Valley eateries.

"So it looks like Brandon hasn't taken over Todd's column – yet," Lauren mused.

"Yeah." Zoe continued to stare at the screen. "Unless the new reviews *have* been written and the website designer just hasn't uploaded them yet."

"Would a designer do that? Or would each member of staff?" Lauren asked.

"I have no idea." Zoe shrugged, then brightened. "But so far it's good news for Gary – no nasty review."

"And good news for us as well," Lauren pointed out.

"Yes – no review is better than a bad review." Zoe shut down the computer and stretched. "I think I'll go to bed now."

"Me, too."

"Brrt!" Annie trotted off toward Lauren's bedroom. She'd been quiet while they scoured the newspaper's website – in fact, she hadn't seemed interested at all. Was that because somehow she knew there weren't any new reviews posted online for the area?

When Lauren reached her bedroom, Annie was already curled up on the bedspread, her eyes closed. Lauren quickly got into her nightgown and slid under the sheet, careful not to disturb Annie. A sleepy "Brrp," was the last sound she heard.

***

Saturday morning, 6.30 a.m. Lauren yawned as she crunched her way through a bowl of granola. Tomorrow she'd definitely sleep in.

"I'm going to crochet this afternoon." Zoe grinned as she bit into a big, juicy strawberry.

"I might put my feet up and read a book," Lauren admitted. "Oh! I can't. I should mow the lawn."

"Yuck!" Zoe wrinkled her nose.

"I know." Lauren crunched extra hard on her cereal. "But Mitch pointed out that it needed cutting."

"Then he can cut it!"

Lauren sighed. One of the joys of being a homeowner was taking care of the garden. She'd rather bake – or relax.

"I mustn't be lazy," she scolded herself aloud.

"Brrp?" Annie wandered into the kitchen, looking bright-eyed and alert. She'd already eaten her breakfast.

"Lauren's going to mow the lawn this afternoon," Zoe told the cat.

Annie gave Lauren a considering look, as if she didn't quite believe the statement.

"Even Annie doesn't think I'll do it." Lauren squared her shoulders and rose from the table. "I have done it before, you know."

"Brrt," Annie replied in a dubious tone.

"You two will see." Lauren placed her dishes in the sink. "We'd better get going."

The three of them walked down the private hallway to the café. Lauren baked raspberry swirl cupcakes – she'd mixed up the batter yesterday afternoon – and Zoe unstacked the chairs and made the space look inviting.

Annie sat in her cat bed, 'supervising'.

When Lauren unlocked the front door, Brandon walked in a minute later. He wore jeans and a t-shirt with a fancy logo on it.

"Hi," Lauren greeted him.

"Hi, Lauren." He grinned. "You're now looking at a bona fide food critic!"

"You got the job?" Zoe looked up from the counter.

"Yep." He looked pleased with himself.

"I hope you're going to give us a good review," Zoe said.

"Can I tell you something in confidence?" Brandon leaned over the countertop. "Todd had written a rough draft of his visit here – and it was all positive – so far. He was just waiting to sample Ed's pastries before he finalized it and posted it online."

"Oh." Lauren bit her lip. "Ed doesn't work on Saturdays so there aren't any pastries today for you to sample."

"No worries." Brandon waved away her concern. "My editor wants me to head back to Sacramento today, anyway. News is a 24/7 business. I'll post what Todd wrote, and add my own observations as well."

"I hope they're good ones!" Zoe said cheerily.

"Brrt," Annie added from the cat bed. She hadn't gotten up to greet Brandon when he'd arrived. Was that because she didn't think he wanted to sit at a table?

"Of course," he assured them. "Your coffee's great, and so are your cupcakes. I'll just put in I was disappointed I couldn't try Ed's famous pastries because they'd sold out when we arrived."

"That's good of you." Lauren smiled.

"We finders of dead bodies have to stick together." He winked at Lauren.

She took a sudden step back, although the counter separated her from Brandon, blanching as the image of Todd's body rose before her eyes.

"Brrt," Annie said in a chiding tone.

"Sorry." Brandon looked embarrassed. "That was in bad taste."

Lauren refrained from saying, "Yes, it was." Sometimes she wished she was outspoken like Zoe. She glanced at her cousin, who had her lips pressed together. Was Zoe resisting temptation to reproach him as well?

"Can we make you a coffee before we go?" Lauren hoped her tone sounded pleasant.

"A mocha would be great." Brandon pulled out his wallet. "The newspaper's put me on expenses, now that I'm taking over the column. Todd handled all that before."

"That's thoughtful of them," Zoe said in a subdued tone.

"Yeah." Brandon ran a hand through his slicked back hair. "Maybe I should get a cupcake to go too – for the road."

"Of course." Lauren gave him a raspberry swirl as well as the mocha. "Here you go."

"Thanks." He gave Lauren ten dollars. "Keep the change."

"Thank you." Lauren plinked the coins into the tip jar on the counter.

Once Brandon left the café, Zoe blew out a large breath. "He certainly seems pleased with himself." She tapped her foot.

"I know." Lauren nodded.

"Brrt!"

They glanced over at Annie's bed. The feline sat up, looking like she agreed with them.

"At least it's good news about our review," Lauren said slowly.

"If we can trust him." Zoe frowned.

"I know what you mean." Lauren sighed. "But let's hope we can take him at his word."

"Deal."

A couple of their regulars came in. Annie hopped down from her bed and trotted over to greet them.

Mid-morning, Lauren had just sat down on the stool behind the counter for a second, when a dapper man in his sixties walked in.

"Brrt!" Annie rushed over to greet him, her plumy tail waving in the air.

"Ach, Annie!" The man bent down stiffly to give her a gentle stroke. "How are you today, Liebchen?"

"Brrt," Annie replied in a chatty tone, slowly leading one of her favorite customers toward a table for two near the counter.

"Hi, Hans." Lauren made her way over to the table. Annie had already jumped on the vacant seat across from him.

"Hello, Lauren." Hans smiled, his eyes crinkling with good humor. "I hope you and Zoe have not had a nasty – how do you say – run-in with that food critic."

"No." Lauren shook her head. "He visited here the other day but I think it went okay." *Apart from finding his dead body the next day.*

"That is *gut*."

"But how did you know about it?" Lauren eyed him quizzically.

"It is all over the town." He gestured to the large glass window near the door. Passersby strolled past the entrance.

"The food critic went everywhere. Here, the burgers at Gary's Burger Diner, there, the steakhouse, the—"

"He went to the steakhouse?"

"*Ja.* Everywhere. Even to the restaurants a couple of towns over."

"You know more than Zoe and I do." Lauren looked at him admiringly.

"It is all anyone talks about at the senior center," Hans admitted, a twinkle in his eye. "*Did you see the food critic here? Did you see him there? I recognized his photo from his website.*' It is big news for a small town. And so many people my age now have phones or these tablets, so they can keep up with their grown-up children on email or social media. And the center has free WiFi."

"That's handy."

"Ja."

Lauren and Hans chatted for a couple more minutes, Annie joining in the conversation with an occasional "Brrt." After taking his order for a cappuccino and a raspberry swirl cupcake, Lauren hurried back to the counter.

"Oh, no." Zoe's expression fell as she glanced toward the door. "Ms. Tobin." A skinny woman in her fifties wearing a skirt and blouse in dull brown walked in.

Annie hopped down from her chair at Hans's table and sauntered over to the *Please Wait to be Seated* sign. She glanced up at the tall woman, then led her to a secluded table near the back.

Ms. Tobin was one of their most difficult customers. Everything had to be just so. And if it wasn't …

But for some reason, Annie always led her to a table. Perhaps the Norwegian Forest Cat discerned Ms. Tobin was lonely, or unhappy, or perhaps both. But Lauren always sensed that Ms. Tobin preferred Annie's brief company to hers or Zoe's when they took her order.

That was another thing. Ms. Tobin expected them to come to her to take her order, whereas Lauren and Zoe usually reserved that special service for the elderly, infirm or otherwise indisposed customers, such as Claire and her toddler daughter Molly.

"I'll go," Lauren said. "You take care of Hans's order."

"Thanks." Zoe flashed her a smile.

Lauren watched Annie trot back to Hans's table. Ms. Tobin did not seem to mind that the feline led her to a table and then departed.

For some customers, the novelty of Annie choosing a table for them was all they wanted, while others enjoyed Annie spending time with them as they drank their coffee and munched on sweet treats.

"What can I get you, Ms. Tobin?" Lauren asked politely, pulling her order pad and pencil out of her apron pocket.

"I'll have a large latte. Now, make sure you give me large. Not small, not regular. And I want two espresso shots in it. Don't give me a large that's full of milk and a single shot. It must have two shots of espresso."

"Of course." Lauren wrote down the order, wondering if this was the fifth or the fifty-fifth time Ms. Tobin had uttered those very words. All their large coffees contained two shots of espresso. She told herself not to take Ms. Tobin's attitude personally.

"What sort of cupcakes and pastries do you have?" Ms. Tobin asked with a frown.

She asked that question every time as well.

"Just raspberry swirls this morning," Lauren answered in a trying-to-be-cheery tone. "Ed doesn't work Saturdays, so there aren't any pastries."

"Only *one* kind of cupcake?" Ms. Tobin looked horrified. "Really, Lauren." She sighed in displeasure. "I *suppose* I'll have a raspberry swirl."

She watched Lauren's pencil scratch on the notepad.

"I do hope you're not interfering with dead bodies, Lauren." Ms. Tobin tutted.

"What?" Lauren's fingers froze on the pencil.

"I heard that you found the food critic's body. Was he going to give you a bad review?" Ms. Tobin looked at her in disapproval.

For a second, Lauren was tempted to make up an outlandish tale just to see the prickly woman's reaction, but she held back. Although she was grateful for every customer, sometimes she wished Ms. Tobin wasn't one of them.

Instead, she forced herself to remain pleasant and to reassure the woman – or at least attempt to – that finding Todd's body was just something that had happened.

"I thought you were going to murder her," Zoe whispered to her as she returned to the counter. Lauren clattered a white china plate before reaching with tongs for a cupcake.

"Was it that obvious?" She glanced at her cousin. "I thought I was doing a good job of staying calm under pressure."

"That's why I hate serving her. I'm sure I'll blurt out something rude." Zoe looked at the order and started steaming milk for the large latte.

"I was tempted to this time." Lauren sighed and looked at her white plastic watch. In a few hours she'd be in the cottage with a good book, Annie in her lap.

Wait. She had to mow the lawn.
Darn.

"I definitely need a cupcake today." Zoe looked at the remaining cupcakes, pulled out a cardboard box, and placed two raspberry swirls inside. "There. Our lunch treat."

"Good idea." Lauren refused to feel guilty. After her run-in with Ms. Tobin, she definitely needed one.

The rest of the morning passed by in a blur. Luckily, Ms. Tobin was the only difficult customer. By lunchtime, Zoe was already stacking the chairs on the tables.

"Brrt!" Annie stood in front of the door to the hallway, looking eager to go home.

"Want to help me crochet this afternoon?" Zoe asked the cat.

"Brrp." Annie tilted her head to one side, as if considering the question.

"Or maybe you want to watch me mow the lawn," Lauren teased.

"Brrt!" Annie's eyes sparkled as she looked up at Lauren. Her lips turned up at the corners, as if she were smiling.

"Oh, I wanted to pick a few leaves of sage for lunch." Lauren hurried through to the kitchen and out the back door. She turned toward the herb garden on the left, then paused.

The shaggy green grass had transformed into a smooth, freshly mown lawn.

Lauren walked over to the waist high white picket fence separating her cottage from the café. The lawn had been cut there as well.

"What the …?" The grass had been long this morning. But how had someone taken care of it without her knowing about it?

"Have you closed?" Mitch Denman asked gruffly. He wore faded blue jeans and a gray t-shirt that hinted at a muscular chest.

Lauren whirled around to face him. He'd silently come around the side of the building while she'd stared at the shorn grass.

"Yes." She self-consciously touched her hair. "I just came out to pick some herbs and saw that—" she gestured toward the smooth lawn.

"Thought you needed a hand." He rocked back on his heels.

"You did this?" She stared up at him.

"Yes."

"But … how?" She furrowed her brow. "I didn't hear a thing."

"My lawnmower's pretty quiet. And I didn't want to disturb you. It looked like you had plenty of customers."

"So you just … here, and my cottage." She waved toward the fence separating the two Victorian buildings.

"Hope you don't mind."

"Mind?" She stifled a nervous giggle. "You've just saved me from a boring afternoon of lawn mowing."

"Glad I could help." His gaze captured hers, his dark brown eyes warm yet slightly guarded.

She glanced away, her gaze landing on the smoothly cut grass.

"I can't believe you did this."

"I know you're busy running the café." He shrugged. "I've got the weekend off, and I don't mind yard work."

"Thank you." She smiled up at him. "You must let me repay you somehow. What about free coffee and cupcakes for the next month?"

"Deal." His eyes crinkled at the corners and his mouth tilted upward.

Lauren gazed at him, her stomach fluttering.

"Lauren, are you okay? We've been waiting – oh!" Zoe stopped in her tracks, Annie skipping around her sneaker clad feet.

The spell was broken.

"Mitch mowed the lawn." Lauren waved her hand toward the grass.

"Brrt." Annie looked up at Mitch in an approving way.

Lauren glanced at the cat and then at Mitch. Had Annie somehow known this was going to happen? Was that why she'd looked like she was smiling when Lauren had come out here?

"He did?" Zoe grinned. "Awesome! Now I don't have to feel guilty for wanting to crochet instead of helping."

"Anytime." Mitch shoved his hands into the back pockets of his jeans. "I'd better get going."

"How's the investigation coming along?" Zoe asked.

"Zoe!"

"We've been wondering." Zoe blinked innocently.

"Mitch has the day off," Lauren told her.

"It's okay." He broke in. "We're working on it. That's all I can say."

"Of course." Lauren nodded.

They watched him depart, Lauren sighing silently as he rounded the corner of the now neat yard. This might have been the first time a guy had done something like this for her without expecting anything in return.

"I told you he likes you." Zoe beamed. "Way to go!" She punched Lauren on the arm.

"Brrt!" Annie chirped in agreement.

"Ow!" Lauren rubbed her forearm. "Not so hard."

"Sorry. Now you can relax this afternoon, just like us."

"Mm." But she didn't know if she could – she might be too busy thinking about Mitch.

CHAPTER 7

"Let's do something." Zoe put down her crochet hook and stretched.

"Like what?" Lauren looked up from her knitting. It was official – she would never finish this scarf.

"Like – like – go salsa dancing! Or ice skating! Or – or – ooh, I know! Let's go to the steakhouse for dinner!" Zoe's eyes sparkled.

"Since I have no idea where we would go salsa dancing or ice skating, the steakhouse does sound tempting," Lauren admitted.

"Brrt!" Annie sat up on the sofa. She'd been snoozing next to Lauren but Zoe's announcement seemed to have woken her. Or perhaps it was the mention of the steakhouse.

"I don't think they allow cats," Lauren told the feline.

"Brrp." Annie scrunched up her face. It looked remarkably like a pout.

"We'll bring a doggy bag – or a pussy bag back for you," Zoe promised.

"Brrt!" Annie's pout disappeared.

"And," Zoe continued, jumping up from the armchair, "I think we should order the wagyu!"

Lauren's knitting needles dropped out of her hands with a clatter.

"But that costs—"

"I know." Zoe nodded. "But we don't often splurge, do we?"

"No," Lauren slowly admitted.

"And," Zoe warmed to her argument, "It could be a once in a lifetime opportunity!"

"But it's one-hundred-and-sixty dollars."

"We could share," Zoe replied.

Lauren hesitated.

"That's only eighty dollars each."

"I think your argument sounded better before you added the cost," Lauren said drily.

"Ple-e-ase?" Zoe batted her eyelashes. "And I bet Annie would love to try expensive wagyu, wouldn't you, sweetie?"

"Brrt!"

Lauren could have sworn Annie batted her eyelashes as well.

She hesitated.

"Okay." Lauren gave in with a sigh.

"Yay!"

"Brrt!"

"Ooh, look at the time." Zoe checked her watch. "It's almost six already. We'd better get ready."

Lauren put her knitting away, then headed to her bedroom. Her stomach had started grumbling, although she didn't know if it was from the mention of expensive steak, or the fact that she hadn't eaten since lunch.

She'd tried to keep her mind on her chick lit novel, but thoughts of Mitch kept intruding, so she'd attempted to continue knitting her scarf, which had been a bit more of a success.

"Brrp." Annie jumped onto the bed.

"We'll bring some steak back for you." Lauren stroked the silky soft silver fur.

Annie bunted her hand, demanding more.

"Are you ready?" Zoe paused in the doorway a few minutes later, wearing black wide-legged pants and a smart blue top.

"Almost." Lauren had chosen a plum wrap dress and black mules.

"Let's go!"

"You're not getting hangry, are you?" Lauren asked.

"Not yet. But I might soon if we don't get going," Zoe admitted.

Lauren and Annie shared a look – uh oh. It wasn't good when Zoe was *hangry*.

They drove to the steakhouse, which was a few blocks away from their cottage.

"We should do this more often," Zoe said as Lauren parked outside. There were a few cars in the lot already and golden outdoor lights invited them to step inside the long, rectangular restaurant.

"I know." Lauren nodded. "As long as it's not eating one- hundred-and-sixty-dollar plates of food all the time." Although her income from the café covered all her living expenses including savings, too many expensive nights out would not be good for her bank account.

"This is a one-time super splurge," Zoe reassured her. "We can do other fun things that don't cost a lot. Like when we went to the casino last month."

"That was fun." Lauren smiled. And she'd won at Bingo.

They entered the building, a hostess greeting them immediately.

"Won't you come this way?" The blonde appeared to be in her thirties, with subtle makeup, and wore a black dress.

They followed her to a table set for two in the middle of the room.

Once they were alone with their menus, Zoe murmured, "That wasn't Kimberly."

"I know. But remember when she was in the café the other day? Before Todd – you know. It sounded like she doesn't work here."

"That's right." Zoe tapped the menu. "Because she was complaining Wayne is never home at night."

Lauren gazed around the room. Three other tables were occupied, but they were all a distance away. The steakhouse looked classy, with white linen tablecloths, low lighting, and soft classical background music.

"No wonder Wayne can charge so much for wagyu," Zoe remarked, glancing at the menu, and then at their surroundings. "He's really set the scene."

"He must be a good businessman," Lauren murmured.

"I think we should get some sides," Zoe decided. "We *are* sharing a steak, after all."

"Not too many," Lauren cautioned.

"Okay, Mom." Zoe grinned.

By the time their waitress arrived to take their order, they'd decided to try the stuffed onions as well as the wagyu, which came with a leek and potato gratin. They'd chosen sparkling water to accompany their meal.

Lauren tried not to feel embarrassed when Zoe asked the waitress for two separate plates. "We're sharing the wagyu," she explained.

"You're not the first." The waitress smiled as she took their menus.

"If we're still hungry after, we can fill up for dessert." Zoe winked at Lauren.

It would be nice to eat a dessert someone else had made, but Lauren decided to keep an eye on her spending.

"We'll see."

"I wonder what they're having." Zoe turned in her chair to watch a family of two adults and two teenagers tuck into their meal. The enticing savory aromas wafted across the room.

"Whatever it is, I hope ours tastes as good as theirs smells," Lauren said.

When their meal arrived, Lauren couldn't wait to try it. By the hangry look on Zoe's face, she was sure her cousin felt the same.

Lauren's plate held a small piece of steak, covered in what had been billed as a light and delicate savory sauce made to enhance the flavor of the wagyu. The waitress set down their side of stuffed onions in the middle of the table

"Is this all we get?" Zoe's mouth parted in disappointment as she stared at the small piece of meat on her plate, along with the gratin and some broccoli.

"We split an eight-ounce steak," Lauren reminded her.

"I just thought it would look a bit bigger. Oh well." Zoe began to cut her meat. "I am now going to steak heaven." She popped a piece in her mouth and chewed. And chewed.

"Well?" Lauren cut up her steak and speared a piece with her fork. She waited for her cousin to speak.

"Don't know," Zoe mumbled around her mouthful of food. She forked up another piece of beef.

Lauren frowned. Her stomach grumbled and she tried her first bite.

A pleasant beefy taste. The sauce was nice, reminiscent of barbecue, but she could not tell the difference between this eighty-dollar piece of steak and the thirty-dollar one she'd had a few months ago in Sacramento.

Perhaps she just wasn't a gastronome.

"Well?" Zoe asked.

Lauren chewed.

"I don't know." She echoed Zoe. "Let's try these." She helped herself to a stuffed onion.

"Yeah." Zoe stabbed at the plate.

The leek and potato gratin accompanying the meat was good, along with the grilled broccoli. So were the stuffed onions, overflowing with rice, bacon, and peppers.

However, Lauren couldn't help thinking she'd just wasted eighty dollars on a small steak.

"Still want dessert?" Lauren asked when they'd both eaten everything on their plates, apart from a small portion of meat she'd set aside for Annie that had escaped the sauce.

"No." Zoe patted her stomach. "Everything filled me up more than I thought."

"Same here." Lauren sipped her water.

"Hello, girls." Wayne suddenly appeared in the dining room, his white chef's outfit making him appear even more solid. A couple of diners looked at him curiously. "I heard you were here."

"Hi, Wayne," Lauren replied.

"So, how was everything?"

Lauren glanced at Zoe.

"Good," they chorused.

"Great, great." Wayne rubbed his hands. "That's what I like to hear. You must have enjoyed it." He glanced at their empty plates.

Lauren couldn't tell him the reason they'd eaten almost every scrap was because they'd been starving.

"Oh, was there something wrong with your steak?" He eyed the portion Lauren had set aside for Annie.

"We need a doggy bag – or a cat bag for Annie." Zoe spoke up.

"I should have guessed." Wayne grinned. "No problem. Let me take care of that for you."

"Thanks." Lauren smiled.

When Wayne departed for the kitchen, Zoe leaned forward. "I hope Annie likes the wagyu more than I did."

"You didn't enjoy it?" Lauren furrowed her brow.

"That's just it. I did enjoy it but I thought I would enjoy it a lot more. Because—"

"Here you go, Lauren." Wayne returned with a neatly wrapped foil parcel.

Zoe drew back and sat up straight in her chair, pretending she hadn't just been speaking.

"Thank you," Lauren replied.

"Can I get you two anything else?" Wayne asked. "We've got chocolate cheesecake as well as a few other desserts."

Lauren glanced at Zoe. It was tempting, but …

"No thanks," they both said at the same time.

"All right." Wayne nodded. "I'll just get the check for you."

He returned to the kitchen.

"Maybe we should talk when we're in the car," Zoe said in a whisper.

"Good idea."

The waitress stopped by a minute later with the bill. Lauren and Zoe split it, and left a tip. After saying goodnight, they headed toward the car. The sun had set but it was still light.

"If that was wagyu then I don't know what the big deal is." Zoe fastened her seatbelt with a harsh click.

"I know what you mean." Lauren sighed. "I hoped it was just me."

"It definitely wasn't you," Zoe reassured her. "I just hope Annie likes it. I was so hungry, I ate it all before remembering to save any for her." A guilty look flashed across her face.

"It's okay." Lauren turned on the ignition and backed out of the space.

"So why did Todd give the steakhouse such a good review a while ago?" Zoe mused as Lauren drove down the street. "He must know what wagyu tastes like, don't you think?"

"He should if he's critiquing it," Lauren replied.

"Maybe Wayne was having a bad night," Zoe suggested. "Or he has a new chef who doesn't know how to cook wagyu. Because I couldn't tell much difference between what we had tonight and an ordinary steak."

CHAPTER 8

At least Annie enjoyed the steak. Lauren watched the Norwegian Forest Cat gobble down the treat as if she hadn't been fed for a few days, when Lauren knew for a fact she'd enjoyed breakfast, lunch, and some kibble that afternoon.

"Maybe we'd better not splurge again for a little while." Zoe had been downcast since they'd returned home. "After buying the yarn for my crochet project, and dinner tonight, I don't have any money left." She opened her red leather wallet. The lined folds were indeed empty.

"I know what you mean." Lauren nodded. "But at least we can say we've tried wagyu."

Zoe made a face. "I think we should stick to coffee and cupcakes."

They both laughed. Annie looked up, her expression enquiring, then returned to her beef.

Lauren's dreams were jumbled that night. First, images of her unfinished red scarf arose, then Mitch, then her plate of wagyu, first covered in sauce, then without. She was glad when the sunlight steaming through her drapes woke her the next morning.

On Sunday, Lauren and Zoe went for a short hike in the nearby Tahoe National Forest. Lauren finished reading her book, barely thinking about Mitch at all that afternoon – well, maybe four times.

On Monday, Lauren and Zoe got the housework out of the way, and checked on Mrs. Finch, who invited them in for coffee.

And then it was Tuesday morning.

"All ready!" Zoe stood behind the counter at 9.30 a.m. The gleaming wooden floorboards looked clean enough to serve coffee and cupcakes on, and Annie sat in her basket, her green eyes alert, as if she waited for her first customer to walk through the door.

"Ed's already making blueberry Danish," Lauren told her, coming out of the swinging kitchen doors.

"After our relaxing weekend, I'm ready to work, work, work." Zoe grinned.

"I know what you mean," Lauren replied.

"Hi, girls." The front door opened with a rush and Claire and her daughter appeared.

"Hi, Claire," Lauren greeted her. "Hi, Molly." She bent down to the stroller.

"Brrt!" Annie jumped down from her bed and trotted toward the toddler.

"Annie!" Molly waved her legs and feet in the air. In her chubby fist she clutched Bear.

"Molly talked about you three all weekend." Claire smiled. "I promised her we'd come and visit you as soon as you were open."

"'ook, Annie." Molly waved her toy in the air. "Bear."

"Molly insisted on bringing Bear today," Claire continued. "She said if she lost it, Annie would find it for her again."

Lauren's heart melted as she watched the blonde toddler gently stroke Annie. The cat seemed to enjoy the child's attention.

"What can we get you?" Lauren asked.

"Do you have any triple chocolate cupcakes?" Claire asked hopefully.

"Yes." Lauren grinned. They were the first treats she'd made that morning.

"Awesome. And a double shot latte. Your coffee is the best."

"Thank you." Satisfaction filled her at the compliment. She strived to create the best experience she could with her menu items.

"Cino!" The little girl turned her attention to Lauren for an instant, then back to Annie.

"No problem." Zoe grinned.

"Won't you two join me?" Claire asked. She glanced around the empty café. "Sometimes I'm desperate for adult conversation. My husband works long hours."

"We'd love to," Zoe said enthusiastically. "We'll sit with you when we bring your order over."

"Annie can show you to a table," Lauren added.

The feline glanced up at Lauren, her ears pricked. She seemed to nod, and trotted toward a table for four in the center of the room.

"How does she do that?" Claire marveled, pushing the stroller after Annie.

"Cat magic," Zoe replied with a giggle.

Lauren and Zoe plated the order, and brought it over to the trio. No other customers had arrived yet. That would worry Lauren normally, but this morning she was looking forward to chatting with Claire.

Annie sat on one of the chairs. Molly stayed in her stroller, and Lauren and Zoe took the remaining two pine chairs.

Claire took her first sip of latte, her eyes closing in appreciation. The aroma of dark cherry, nuts, and spices wafted from her cup.

"Exactly what I needed." She set down the mug.

"Cino!" Molly smacked her lips together after tasting her own drink, a chocolate speckled foam mustache coating her upper lip. Her mother grinned when she caught sight of it.

"What made you move here?" Zoe asked curiously.

"My husband's job," Claire replied, forking up a bite of triple chocolate cupcake. "He worked for a newspaper in L.A. for years – so did I – and then he was offered a promotion in Sacramento, on one of the company's other papers. It made financial sense to take it."

"So he commutes every day?" Lauren asked.

"Yes." Claire nodded. "We decided to buy a house here, rather than in Sacramento. The elementary school has great reviews, and I've always liked the idea of living in a small town."

"Do you still work for the newspaper?" Zoe asked curiously

"No. I quit when I was pregnant. I wanted to focus on the baby, not on who was currying favor with my boss so they could get the best assignments."

"Oh," Lauren murmured.

"My husband's on the marketing side, so he didn't have to put up with all that. And we were worried about the crime rate in L.A., so when the opportunity came up for the Sacramento job, he took it."

"That's understandable." Zoe nodded.

"Brrt," Annie said.

"But now …" she hesitated. "With Todd Fane killed, right here—" she let out a big breath. "Do you think the police know who did it?"

"No," Lauren replied. "I mean, we don't know if the police know."

"I asked the detective on Saturday," Zoe chimed in. "He said they were investigating."

"Todd wasn't the nicest person, but I didn't think he deserved to die," Claire said.

Lauren's eyes widened. So did Zoe's.

"You knew him?" Zoe asked.

"Yes." Claire nodded, then looked embarrassed. "Maybe I shouldn't have said anything."

"How did you know him?" Lauren asked after a couple of seconds.

"I used to work with him – in L.A.," Claire admitted.

"Wow!" Zoe stared at her.

"It was a long time ago."

Lauren glanced over at the toddler. She'd finished her babycino and was gently patting Annie.

"Did you know he was here, reviewing restaurants?" Lauren asked her.

"No." Claire forked up another bite of cupcake. "I only found out later, when I read about it in the newspaper."

That made sense.

"Does he work for the same newspaper as your husband?" Zoe asked.

Claire hesitated. "Yes."

"Who do you think did it?" Zoe leaned forward. "Did Todd have any enemies?"

"Zoe!" Lauren hissed.

"Well, he didn't seem to mind making them. I don't think Todd would let anything stand in his way career wise. I was just glad that I wasn't on the food beat with him," Claire replied. "I ended up in fashion and I had my own co-workers to deal with. Our paths didn't cross that much."

"But if he worked in a city like L.A., why would he move to Sacramento, which is smaller?" Zoe frowned.

Claire shrugged. "I don't know. I'd left by then. Maybe it was actually a promotion, like my husband's move was?"

"I guess." Zoe's tone was a little doubtful.

"Perhaps the Sacramento paper wanted an experienced food critic," Lauren suggested. "They might have offered him more money than he was making in L.A."

"And the cost of living in Sacramento might be lower than L.A.," Zoe said thoughtfully. "So it could have been a good move financially for him."

"I doubt Todd wouldn't do something that didn't benefit him in some way," Claire told them.

"Apart from being murdered." Zoe shuddered.

***

"I still think it's strange," Zoe said a few hours later. "What are the odds that an old co-worker of Todd's moves to the small town where he winds up murdered? And, that same co-worker's husband works – worked – on the same newspaper as Todd?"

"I understand what you're saying," Lauren replied. The lunch rush had been brief today and now they had a few minutes to chat. "But Claire said she moved here two months ago. How would she even know that he was coming to Gold Leaf Valley?"

"By reading his food column," Zoe told her. "Or gossip around the water cooler at the paper. Her husband could have told her over dinner one night."

"But why would she care about Todd being here?" Lauren asked. "It didn't sound as if she was a fan of his."

"Exactly! So she'd keep track of him by reading his column, asking her husband about him, and discovering which areas Todd was covering."

"But why?" Lauren repeated. "What would be her motive to keep tabs on Todd?"

"Because – because …" Zoe trailed off. "Huh. But you have to admit it's a huge coincidence she's now living in the same town where he was killed, and that her husband worked for the same newspaper."

"I do," Lauren told her. "But I just can't see Claire as a killer. Her daughter Molly is adorable, and Annie seems to enjoy their company."

"Brrt," Annie confirmed. She looked over at them from her cat bed.

"Well, Annie *is* a good judge of character," Zoe said slowly. "Apart from Ms. Tobin. Why she persists in showing that woman to a table beats me."

"Maybe Annie can see something in her we can't," Lauren replied, giving the Norwegian Forest Cat a fond look.

"I guess." Zoe sighed. "But we still haven't done much about finding out who the killer is. Even Mrs. Finch seemed disappointed we didn't have any inside information at crochet club."

"Don't you mean knitting and crochet club?" Lauren teased. "I'm still working on my scarf."

"That's what I meant." Zoe grinned.

They tidied the counter, Annie settling in her basket for a snooze. The café was strangely quiet, their customers returning to work or home.

Tuesday wasn't as busy as the rest of the week, but still …

Lauren gazed into space, once again wondering why Brandon hadn't heard Todd's murderer, since he'd been in the motel room next door, when the front door swung open.

"Brrp?" Annie lifted her head. Her eyes widened, and she jumped down from the bed.

Lauren blinked, her trance broken. Mitch stood in the doorway, wearing what she now thought of as his business attire – dark slacks and a dress shirt – this time, pewter gray.

"Hi." She scolded herself for sounding breathless.

"Hey." He walked toward the counter.

Annie joined him.

"Brrp?" she repeated.

"Ah – hello?" He peered down at the cat.

"I think she's asking if you'd like a table or if you're ordering to go," Lauren explained.

"To go." He nodded.

"Brrt." Annie sounded a little disappointed as she ambled back to her bed.

"I didn't think she liked me much." Mitch stared at Annie's retreating form. "But she seemed friendlier just now."

"I think she's aware that you mowed our lawn," Lauren said. "She knows I don't like doing it."

"Huh." He shook his head as if to clear it. "Are all cats like that?"

"Maybe," Lauren replied, although to her, Annie was the most intelligent and sweetest cat in the world.

"I thought I'd get a latte," Mitch said. "And a cupcake, if you have any left." He eyed the glass case containing the baked goods. Several cakes were left, along with two blueberry Danishes.

"Of course." Lauren smiled as she picked up a pair of tongs. "I have triple chocolate or lemon poppyseed."

"Which one do you recommend?"

"The triple chocolate." A couple more customers had raved about it earlier, making Lauren's day.

"It sounds good."

Lauren steamed the milk for the latte as the espresso machine growled and hummed. She searched her brain, but couldn't think of any small talk.

"Ed said to remind you he's leaving now because of his dental appointment." Zoe burst in through the swinging kitchen doors.

"That's right." Lauren had forgotten about it.

"Got any news about the murder?" Zoe asked Mitch.

"Not that I can share," Mitch replied.

"That's too bad." Zoe sounded disappointed. "When do you think you'll catch the killer?"

"Zoe!" Lauren frowned.

"Soon, I hope," Mitch answered. "We want to make sure we arrest the right person."

"You do know that Brandon returned to Sacramento, don't you?" Zoe asked as Lauren put a lid on the latte cup.

"Yes, I do." Mitch dug into his pocket for his wallet.

"On the house," Lauren told him. "I said on Saturday—"

"I know." He smiled. It transformed his face. "But I didn't want to take advantage."

"I meant what I said," Lauren told him. "Free coffee and cupcakes for the next month."

"I think that's totally worth mowing the lawn for," Zoe observed.

"Two lawns," Lauren reminded her.

"Oh, yeah."

"I was planning on making vanilla cupcakes tomorrow," Lauren told him shyly, aware of his liking for that particular treat.

"Then I'll definitely come back tomorrow."

CHAPTER 9

"He's reviewed us!" Zoe called out from the living room the next morning.

"Brandon?" Lauren and Annie looked at each other over the breakfast table. Annie sat on a chair while Lauren munched on her granola.

"What does it say?" Lauren's stomach swirled, jumbling up the oats and dried fruit she'd just eaten.

"It's all good," Zoe assured her, walking into the kitchen with the laptop. "He says the coffee and cupcakes are great but he was disappointed he couldn't try Ed's pastries. Ooh – he also mentions Annie. Says she's a cute cat and that customers love her hostess role."

"Show me?"

Zoe placed the laptop on the kitchen table. "See?" She indicated the screen.

"Brrt?" Annie nudged Lauren's shoulder.

"Here." Zoe pointed at the device. "Look, Annie, there's your name." She tapped the screen.

"Brrt." Annie sounded pleased.

"That's a relief." Lauren's stomach settled back to normal.

"Hopefully his review will give us some new customers." Zoe grinned. "And I know one customer who's coming in today, so you'd better get those vanilla cupcakes in the oven."

"Who's the boss now?" Lauren teased, her cheeks suddenly hot. Just the mention of Mitch's name made her blush. She had to get it together.

"Keep plying him with lattes and cupcakes and he might continue to mow the lawn forever," Zoe kidded.

"You're terrible!" Lauren tutted, but secretly she wondered what it would be like if Zoe's words became true. And not just for the benefit of not needing to do yardwork.

After finishing breakfast, the three of them walked down the hallway to the café.

Lauren mixed up the vanilla cupcakes first, wanting to make sure they were ready by the time Mitch stopped by.

Soon after, Ed arrived, donning his big apron and nodding to Lauren before checking the ingredients for his pastries. He didn't like to be interrupted while working.

If Brandon ever reviewed them again, she just hoped they had some of Ed's pastries to tempt him with. Ed's skill with pastry was one of the reasons she had so many customers – along with Annie's hostess duties.

"Hey Ed, did you see our review?" Zoe popped her head into the kitchen. "Brandon loved our coffee and cupcakes."

"Good," Ed grunted, shaping a round of dough on the clean counter.

"Just wait until he tries one of your pastries," Zoe continued. "Hey, I know! Why don't I email Brandon and tell him to come back any time he likes to try one of Ed's specialties?"

"Good idea," Lauren told her cousin. She glanced at Ed, working the pastry, and back at Zoe.

Zoe nodded, miming zipped lips, and went back into the café.

Once the cupcakes were in the oven, Lauren slipped into the café as well.

"Everything's ready and it's not even 9.30." Zoe sat at the counter, one leg swinging against the metal leg of the stool. "Should we open a little early?"

"Why not?" Lauren unlocked the front door. No customers clamoring to enter at 9.15. Darn.

Annie strolled around the room, as if checking all the chairs and tables were accounted for.

"I wonder when Mitch will come in today." Zoe tapped her cheek.

"Make sure there's a vanilla cupcake for him in case he comes in this afternoon," Lauren said.

"Will do." Zoe giggled. "You two are so cute. I just hope I'm not one hundred by the time he asks you out."

"Stop that." Lauren stifled a nervous giggle.

"You must know he likes you by now. He—"

The door opened. Gary strode in.

"I couldn't believe my luck when I saw you were open already." He smiled at Lauren and Zoe. Annie gave a grumble when she noticed he stood at the counter and not at the *Please Wait to be Seated* sign.

"What can we get you?" Lauren asked, her fingers poised on the register.

"A large cappuccino would be great." He pulled out his wallet. "Hey, I saw that the new food critic posted a review for this place."

"Yep, we read it this morning," Zoe confirmed. "Hopefully it will bring in some extra business."

"Did you get a review yet?" Lauren asked.

"No." Gary frowned and shook his head. "But right now I think that's a good thing."

"Definitely." Zoe nodded so hard, her brunette pixie bangs brushed her eyes. "Ooh, we should definitely have burgers for dinner one night." She turned to Lauren.

"Good idea," Lauren replied. She'd always had a great experience there, and it wouldn't break her bank account either. "What about next week?"

"You girls are welcome any time." Gary waved away the change Lauren tried to give him. "Put it in the tip jar."

"Thanks." Zoe beamed.

Lauren clinked the coins into the jar on the counter.

Gary checked his chunky silver watch. "I've got to get back to the diner." His mouth tightened. "Cindy was so upset about what happened with that – *critic* – that she needed to take a couple of days off. I still can't believe what that creep tried to do to her." He shook his head as he left the café.

"Ooh." Zoe stared after Gary.

"I know." Lauren nodded. "He still seems angry about what happened."

"I would be too." Zoe paused. "Hey, I should have enough tip money by next week to cover a burger and fries." She tried to lighten the mood.

"You don't have any money at all?" An image of Zoe's empty wallet flashed in front of Lauren's eyes. "Do you want me to pay you early?"

"No, I'm fine." Zoe waved away the offer. "I just don't have any money in my wallet, that's all. I've got some in the bank. I'm just trying to leave it in there." She sighed.

"Maybe we shouldn't have splurged at the steakhouse Saturday night."

"I hear you." Lauren looked at Zoe's regretful expression. She touched her cousin's arm. "But I'm glad we did, despite how much it cost." She realized she meant it. "You were right. Sometimes we should do something fun."

"Next week burgers at Gary's, then." Zoe cheered up. "Good food and it's affordable."

"You're on."

CHAPTER 10

That afternoon, Mitch stopped by. Lauren willed herself to remain calm as she served him. Annie ambled up to him inquiringly, but when he told her he was getting take-out, she wandered over to one of her regular customers instead, and joined them at their table.

As she placed his vanilla cupcake in a cardboard tray, Lauren peeked up at him from underneath her eyelashes. He looked as business-like as he usually did (apart from Saturday when he mowed her lawn).

She handed him his latte, a shiver racing along her spine when her fingers grazed his.

"Thanks." He smiled briefly. A ringtone sounded, and he dug his phone out of his pocket. "Sorry. I've got to take this."

"No problem." Lauren watched him walk out of the café, juggling his coffee, cupcake, and phone. Maybe Zoe was right – her cousin would be one hundred by the time Mitch asked Lauren out – which would make Lauren one-hundred-and one.

"Only two days 'til crochet and knitting club. I can't wait to show Mrs. Finch how much crochet I've done this week," Zoe said enthusiastically a few minutes later when she joined Lauren at the counter.

"Oh, that reminds me. I'm almost out of wool for my scarf. I need to buy some more."

"I can take care of everything." Zoe made a shooing motion. "Go to the handmade shop before it closes."

"Are you sure?" Lauren scanned the room. Only a few customers ate, drank, and chatted at the tables. Annie sat with Pastor Mike, who ran the local Episcopal church.

"Go!" Zoe made a shooing motion once more.

Lauren grabbed her purse and departed before she could persuade herself to change her mind. It wasn't often that she left the coffee shop while they were open.

She breathed in a lungful of fresh spring air. The afternoon sun shone and a cool breeze ruffled her hair. It did feel good to be outside.

Lauren hurried to the store. She'd just buy her yarn and get back to the café. She was so busy wondering if she would ever finish her scarf that she nearly walked past the small shop.

A bell tinkled as she entered the store. An array of colorful wool met her eyes, piled high on the shelves. Oh no! She didn't know which shade of red she needed. Zoe had bought it for her, and she hadn't thought to bring the wool with her to match it.

Lauren approached the counter. A woman in her forties with curly brown hair operating the register spoke to the only other customer.

"I'm sorry, but this card is declined."

"It can't be," the slim, tall woman wailed. "Try it again."

"Okay," the clerk said doubtfully. She swiped the card once more. "No. I'm sorry."

Lauren winced with sympathy for the customer. She frowned and looked at her more closely. Honey colored hair hitting her jawline. Was it Kimberly, Wayne's wife?

"What am I going to do? I need all this." The woman who might be Kimberly scooped up the skeins of yarn and clutched them to her chest. "I wanted to knit a sweater in cable stitch!"

"We also take cash," the clerk replied.

"I don't have any. I pay for everything with a card. My husband said he'd paid the credit card bill last week. Please—" the woman pushed the card across the counter to the clerk "—try again."

"Okay."

Lauren thought the clerk sounded patient.

A minute later, the clerk shook her head. "It's still declined."

"I can't believe this." The woman sounded distraught.

"Maybe you could check with your husband?" the clerk suggested. "He might have forgotten to pay the credit card bill."

"That would be just like him," the woman fumed. She turned to go, still clutching the wool. Her eyes widened. "Lauren."

"Kimberly." She'd been right. Her heart went out to the older woman.

"What are you doing here?" Kimberly made an attempt to laugh.

"I need some more wool for my scarf."

"I'm going to knit a sweater." Her eyes flashed. "*If* my husband paid the credit card bill."

"Ma'am—" the clerk began.

Kimberly swiveled. "You'll put this aside for me, won't you?" She tumbled the skeins onto the counter. "Until I can get everything straightened out with my card."

The clerk's gaze flickered to Lauren and then back to Kimberly. "Of course."

"It's Kimberly Rymer."

Kimberly turned to go, then paused. "Oh, Lauren, my husband told me you and Zoe had dinner at the steakhouse the other night. How was everything?"

"It was great," Lauren replied politely. What else could she say? That the wagyu had been disappointing?

"That's wonderful." Kimberly smiled, as if she hadn't just been embarrassed about her declined card. "You two must come again soon. I'll tell Wayne to give you a twenty percent discount."

"Oh, that's kind of you, but you mustn't—"

"Nonsense." Kimberly waved a hand in the air. "It's all settled. I'm sure Wayne can find a table for you anytime, even during a busy evening."

"Thanks," Lauren replied, not sure what else to say.

Kimberly exited the shop, the bell tinkling her departure. Lauren smiled hesitantly at the clerk, explaining her wool dilemma.

"Oh, no problem," the clerk reassured her. "I remember Zoe." She grinned. "She was very enthusiastic about your knitting venture. And her crochet project. I remember which wool she bought both times."

Lauren purchased two more balls, trusting that would be enough. Hopefully she would never be in the mortifying position of having her card declined, although she preferred paying with old-fashioned cash.

"That's a lot of yarn," Lauren commented, eyeing Kimberly's stash. Skeins of cream fiber dotted the counter.

"You'd be surprised at how much you need for some projects," the clerk replied, placing Lauren's purchase in a brown paper bag. "I just hope Kimberly claims it soon – it's a very popular item. If I run out of stock on the shelf and she hasn't come back for it …"

"I understand," Lauren said, sympathizing with the clerk – and Kimberly.

As she left the store, an image flashed in front of her. Kimberly sitting down at the café, bags of purchases surrounding her chair. She'd just visited the outlet mall.

Did Kimberly have a shopping addiction? Or was Lauren making too much of it? Just because Lauren tried to be careful with her purchases most of the time didn't mean other people had to be.

Or was it just like the clerk had suggested – Wayne, Kimberly's husband, had forgotten to pay the credit card bill?

***

The next day, Brandon entered the café, halting at the *Please Wait to be Seated* sign.

"Brrt." Annie trotted toward him and looked up at him coyly.

"Hi, Annie." He grinned down at her.

"Hi." Lauren headed toward him. The café was half full and nobody was attempting to attract her attention. "Thank you for your—"

"Review," Zoe finished, rounding the counter. "We read it online the other day."

"I think Annie loved what you wrote about her," Lauren said, glancing down at the Norwegian Forest Cat.

"Brrt!"

"It was all true," Brandon replied, looking pleased.

"Did you get my email about Ed's pastries?" Zoe asked.

"Yep. That's why I'm here." He looked over at the glass case hopefully. "If you have any left."

"You're in luck. We have one apricot Danish."

"Awesome!" He grinned.

"Brrt."

"I think Annie wants to show you to a table," Lauren told him.

"Thanks, Annie." He followed the feline to a table near the counter.

"Oops, we didn't ask if he wanted coffee," Zoe said.

"We can ask him in a sec." Lauren plated the pastry, and with Zoe following on her heels, took it over to Brandon.

"Coffee?" Zoe asked.

"A mocha would be great," he replied.

Annie perched on the other chair at the four-seater table.

"I'll make it." Zoe zipped back to the counter.

Something had been troubling Lauren for a while, and now

Brandon's presence brought it to the forefront of her mind. Surely it was safe to talk about it? They were in a public place, and the soft buzz of conversation provided an illusion of privacy.

"You look like you want to ask me something," Brandon said, a fork in his hand.

"You're right," Lauren replied ruefully. "I keep thinking about that morning – when I found Todd's – Todd. You said you heard me knocking on his door and that's why you came over to see what was going on. But you didn't hear the killer."

"Yeah." Brandon looked regretful. "I told the cops why that was. I was listening to music on my phone and I had my earbuds in. I like it really loud, and there are some good drum solos. That's why I didn't hear the murderer." His mouth twisted. "I just wish I had. Maybe I could have stopped him – or her."

"Oh, I'm sorry." That explained why Brandon's hair had looked a little mussed at the time.

"I feel like I failed Todd. If I hadn't been listening to my music—"

"You mustn't blame yourself," Lauren told him.

"Brrt," Annie agreed.

"You couldn't have known what was going to happen that morning."

"You're right." He nodded. "But I think it will take me a while to process it all."

Zoe arrived with Brandon's mocha. "Have I interrupted anything?" She studied their serious expressions.

"It's all good," Brandon assured her. "I was just telling Lauren the reason I didn't hear Todd's killer was because I was listening to loud music wearing earbuds."

"Oh." Zoe looked relieved. "That's one mystery solved, then."

"Yeah." Brandon nodded. "Not the main one, though."

There was a brief silence.

"Okay." Zoe glanced at the three of them again. "So why are you back here in Gold Leaf Valley? I mean, we're glad you came to try Ed's pastries, but you didn't drive all this way from Sacramento just to do that, did you?"

"No," Brandon replied. "I'm here to review the local steakhouse. Todd had it on his list before he – you know – and my editor wants me to review it again. And I can't find Todd's notes for Gary's Burger Diner, so I'm going back there again, too."

"Wayne's steakhouse got a good review last time." Zoe tapped her cheek.

"Yeah." Brandon nodded. "Todd seemed really impressed with it."

"Were you working with him back then?" Lauren asked.

"No. It was just before my time. But Todd told me he likes – liked – updating his reviews when he could, and it seemed like a good idea to critique other places in the area too,

184

like your café. Get a lot done in one location in a few days."

"It's all about content and clicks these days, isn't it?" Zoe asked.

"Yeah." Brandon nodded.

"We had dinner at the steakhouse the other night," Zoe told him.

"How did you like it?" he asked.

"Mm." Lauren tried to be diplomatic.

"We had the wagyu," Zoe confessed. "And I'm afraid—"

"We didn't think it was worth one hundred and sixty dollars per serve," Lauren felt compelled to say.

"We split it," Zoe admitted.

Brandon frowned. "I've only tasted wagyu once in Sacramento and it was so tender, it just melted in my mouth. So it will be interesting to see if the steakhouse wagyu lives up to Todd's previous review."

"Let us know," Zoe said. "Maybe Wayne was having a bad night when we were there."

"Will do." Brandon bit into the Danish. A minute later, he grinned. "Ed is mighty talented."

"So you liked it?" Zoe asked.

"I loved it!" Brandon grinned. "I'll update your review with a paragraph about this apricot Danish and post it as soon as I can."

"That would be great," Lauren said.

"Brrt!" Annie agreed.

They all laughed.

CHAPTER 11

The next morning, Friday, Zoe was on tenterhooks, waiting for Brandon to report back about his dinner at the steakhouse.

"He might be busy," Lauren told her cousin when Zoe had mixed up her second order by ten o'clock. "Maybe he doesn't have time to stop by before he goes back to Sacramento."

"But I'm saving him two of Ed's pastries," Zoe replied.

"Does he know that?"

"No," Zoe admitted ruefully. "The thought popped in my mind this morning when I was having breakfast."

"It was a good thought." Lauren smiled. "I'm curious as well."

"I think Annie is, too." Zoe flicked a glance over at the pink cat bed, where Annie groomed herself. So far, it had been a quiet morning.

Would Mitch come in again for complimentary coffee and cupcakes? Lauren hoped so, although she hated the fact that she felt shy and self-conscious around him.

One hour later, Brandon entered the café.

"Brrt!" Annie trotted over to him.

"Hi, Annie." He smiled down at her.

"Well?" Zoe rushed over to him. "How was the steakhouse?"

"Would you two like a table?" Lauren teased.

"That might be a good idea," Brandon replied.

Annie led them to a small table near the counter – business had picked up and there weren't many seats left.

"You tell Zoe and I'll man the counter," Lauren said.

Zoe plopped down on a pine chair, Annie following suit. Both of them looked at Brandon expectantly.

"Can I get you anything, Brandon?" Lauren asked.

"I've saved two of Ed's pastries for you," Zoe told him. "And it wasn't easy." She gestured at the customers eating and drinking at the other tables.

"I'll take them to go," Brandon told them. "And I'd love a latte if you're not too busy."

"Coming right up." Lauren hurried to the counter.

She watched Zoe say something to Brandon. She could make out the words "steakhouse", "menu", and "sides." The hissing noise of the milk wand drowned out anything else.

After making the latte in record time, she rushed back to the table, placing the beverage in front of Brandon.

"I told him not to say anything about the wagyu until you were here," Zoe assured her.

"Thanks." Lauren smiled. She'd been curious about Brandon's verdict as well.

"Brrt," Annie chirped suddenly, her gaze focused on the front door.

Lauren turned. Wayne strode toward the *Please Wait to be Seated* sign.

"You stay here," Lauren told the feline. "I'll help Wayne."

"Brrt." Annie looked pleased at not having to miss out on hearing about Brandon's experience last night.

"Hi, Wayne." Lauren approached him.

"Hey, Lauren." He glanced around the busy space. "Do you have a small table for me? Otherwise I can get my order to go."

"I'm sure I can find something for you." She gazed around the room, wondering where Annie would seat him. There was a table for two in the corner near the counter, but not too close to Brandon and Zoe.

"Follow me." She led the way to the corner table.

As they passed Brandon and Zoe, she heard Zoe utter, "wagyu" and saw

Brandon nod. She'd have to ask Zoe
for the details later. Brandon mightn't
have time to wait until she was
finished serving Wayne.

"What can I get you?" Lauren
asked once Wayne sat down.

He picked up the menu from the
table. "I might need a minute to
decide." His gaze flickered to
Brandon and Zoe. "That guy visited
the steakhouse last night. Is he a
friend of your cousin's?"

"Something like that," Lauren
replied diplomatically. Was it a secret
that Brandon was a food critic?
Todd's identity hadn't been. But …
she didn't know if Brandon was
supposed to be incognito when he
reviewed restaurants now, or not. It
was probably best not to say anything
more.

"I'll just go look at the cakes in the
glass case," Wayne told her.

"Of course."

Lauren hurried back to Brandon's
table. "What have I missed?"

"I was just about to tell Zoe. I don't know if Wayne had another bad evening, but the wagyu was terrible last night."

"Really?" Zoe leaned forward, her eyes wide.

"Yeah."

Out of the corner of her eye, Lauren saw Wayne walk toward the glass counter to look at the cupcakes available and the few pastries that were left.

"It tasted nothing like the wagyu I had a few months ago," he continued. "In fact, for some reason it reminded me of Angus beef. And serving that sauce with it! If you want people to appreciate the richness of wagyu, don't cover it up in sauce. Have some sauce on the side if you must include it."

"Annie liked the small amount of wagyu I brought home for her," Lauren said, glancing at the Norwegian Forest Cat.

"Brrt." Annie licked her lips.

Brandon chuckled. "I know I'm just starting out in the critiquing business, but honestly, it tasted like good old steak to me."

"It wasn't wagyu?" Zoe's expression fell.

"I'm not saying that," Brandon replied hastily. "Only someone with more experience than me could say that for sure. I doubt Todd would have given a decent review for something that wasn't good. He was a stickler for things like that. He told me that's how you develop a good reputation as a critic. Don't let anything slide."

"Huh." Zoe frowned. "So what happened to Wayne's wagyu?"

"I don't know." Brandon shook his head. "A bad supplier maybe? It happens. Chefs should taste their food, but if Wayne hasn't been trying the wagyu lately, and it looks similar to what he served before, that would be one explanation."

"That could be the answer," Lauren said. She glanced around the café, feeling guilty for keeping Wayne waiting so long. She rose, intending to hurry over to his table to take his order, when she saw him head toward the front door.

"Wayne!" She jogged after him.

He turned and tapped his watch. "Sorry, Lauren, I've got to go." He looked regretful. "My wife called. She wants me to pick up something from the supermarket."

"No problem," Lauren assured him ruefully. She shouldn't have let curiosity get the better of her and ignored a customer for a few minutes.

"What was that all about?" Zoe asked when Lauren headed back to Brandon's table.

"Wayne had to get something for his wife," Lauren said. She turned to Brandon. "I'd better go back to the counter. I can handle the customers if Zoe wants to stay."

"Brandon has to go in a sec, anyway." Zoe rose. "Stop by anytime," she told him.

"Brrt," Annie confirmed.

"I might just do that." He grinned. "Your cupcakes are amazing, Lauren. So is your coffee. And Ed's pastries, of course."

"Thank you." Lauren beamed.

They waved goodbye to him when he left, Annie staring after him.

"I think Annie's a fan," Zoe teased as the cat ambled back to her bed.

"He was very complimentary about her in his review."

"At least we know that he's not the killer," Zoe said.

"I'm glad," Lauren told her.

"And I can't believe he knew about Todd propositioning Cindy like that – threatening to give Gary's burgers a bad review if she wasn't "nice" to him."

"I know." Lauren nodded. "I don't think he's that sort of person."

"He's so …" Zoe sighed. "If only he were five years older, he'd be perfect for me."

"Maybe you can crochet the perfect man," Lauren teased.

"There's a thought." A gleam appeared in Zoe's brown eyes. "Can you imagine if that were possible?"

"Who would you create?"

"Someone interesting, and yummy to look at, and …" Zoe tailed off. "I think I'd have to give it some more thought." She glanced at the front door. "Don't look now, but *your* perfect man has just walked in."

Lauren glanced toward the entrance. Mitch stood in the entrance, wearing charcoal slacks and a blue dress shirt. Her cheeks glowed. Darn.

***

On Monday night, Lauren and Zoe decided to get burgers for dinner.

"I've made enough in tips." Zoe shook her wallet stuffed with silver coins and a few dollar bills. It jingled. "Even after I split the proceeds with Ed."

"That's great." Lauren smiled.

"Brrt!" Annie added.

"We'll bring you back a burger," Lauren promised the cat.

"Brrt!" Annie licked her lips.

"Ooh! I forgot to tell you I saw Brandon's new review for the steakhouse this afternoon." Zoe tapped Lauren's arm.

"What did it say?" Lauren asked.

"It's not good." Zoe shook her head.

"Really?" Lauren swiveled and stared at her cousin.

"Yeah." Zoe nibbled her lip. "It's not a super terrible review, but Brandon mentions the fact that he wasn't impressed with the wagyu."

"Oh."

"Yeah."

"At least he's being honest." Lauren tried to find the bright side. But she wondered how Wayne would feel when he read the critique of his restaurant.

"You should read it," Zoe told her.

"I will. Maybe when we come home."

"Good idea." Zoe patted her stomach. "I'm starting to get hungry."

Lauren fed Annie an early dinner, careful not to give her too much since later she would enjoy the meat patty Lauren planned to bring home for her.

Zoe zoomed around the cottage, getting ready.

Lauren brushed her hair and glanced at her appearance in the mirror. There were a few more golden hints in her brown hair – was that because she and Zoe had spent more time outside last weekend, hiking?

She wondered if Mitch had noticed, and then told herself to stop thinking about him. She wasn't successful.

Gary's Burger Diner was just down the block. Zoe chatted about her crochet project, Lauren listening absently. The police still hadn't found

Todd's killer. Mitch had been close-mouthed when he'd dropped by the café last week for his complimentary cupcake and coffee. She understood that. But she wished Mitch would catch the murderer.

"I'm starving!" Zoe opened the large glass door of the restaurant. The eatery was all stainless steel and glass, but had a pleasant vibe.

Lauren glanced at her watch – six p.m.

"That's what you said at lunch," she teased Zoe.

"Yep," her cousin admitted cheerfully.

Lauren's stomach rumbled as well. She spied Cindy at the hostess station.

"Hi, guys." Cindy approached them, a smile on her face. "Would you like a table or are you getting take-out?"

"We'd love a table," Zoe told her.

"This way."

Cindy led the way to a two-seater table in the middle of the room. "This is my section."

"Cool." Zoe grinned.

"How's everything going after … you know?" Lauren kept her voice down, although the eatery wasn't very busy. Only a few other tables were occupied, and none close by.

"Gary's been great," Cindy said. "He held a big staff meeting and told us that if we ever felt uncomfortable with a customer or a co-worker to let him know immediately. And then he told me privately I should have come to him right away, when Todd was in here. He said he would have taken care of him."

Lauren and Zoe glanced at each other.

Exactly what would have Gary done to "take care" of the food critic?

"I'm glad everything is okay here," Lauren told her.

"So am I." Cindy handed them menus. "Let me know when you're ready to order. Gary's got a new burger." She pointed to the top of the menu. "It's called the smoky barbecue special, and it's awesome! He mixes a special sauce into the meat patty, and then adds more on top."

"It sounds yummy." Zoe stared at the description. "I'll definitely try that. And fries. And a chocolate shake."

"I'll have the same," Lauren said. Her stomach growled. She just hoped Zoe and Cindy couldn't hear it. "And I promised Annie I'd bring her back a burger – a plain meat patty?"

"Of course." Cindy scratched the requests on her order pad. "You guys are going to love Gary's new creation," Cindy promised them. "Won't be long!"

While they waited, Lauren glanced around the room. An elderly couple sat at a corner table, while a young family shared a larger table near them.

"I'm glad we came here," Zoe confided.

"Me too." Lauren relaxed in the stainless-steel chair which was surprisingly comfortable. Soft folk rock music played in the background while the occasional clatter from the kitchen punctuated the music's rhythm.

"If Cindy says the new burger is awesome, then I know it will be," Zoe continued.

"True." Lauren nodded. Whenever they'd eaten here, Cindy's recommendations had always been spot on.

"Cindy seems to have recovered from her encounter with Todd," Zoe remarked. "Which is good."

"Definitely." Lauren nodded.

"I just hope—" Zoe lowered her voice and leaned across the table "— that Gary didn't actually do anything to take care of Todd."

The tantalizing smell of beef cooking wafted out from the kitchen.

"Here are your shakes." Cindy suddenly appeared with two large thick shakes. "Your burgers should be ready in a few minutes."

"Thanks." Zoe leaned back in her chair and unwrapped her straw, the paper rustling. She sucked on the dense chocolate liquid. "Mmm."

Lauren tried hers, closing her eyes in appreciation. The mixture of ice-cream, milk, and syrup melted in her mouth in a river of chocolate goodness.

"Hi, girls."

Lauren's eyelids flew open.

Wayne stood at their table.

"Oh – hi, Wayne," Lauren managed.

"Hi," Zoe said, blinking.

"What are you two doing? Having dinner?" He sent a flickering glance at their table, empty apart from their thick shakes.

"Yes." Lauren nodded. "Just waiting for our burgers."

"So am I." He laughed. "I ordered take-out, and then saw you two over here. It's my night off from the steakhouse. Hey, Lauren, my wife told me she bumped into you at that shop that sells the wool."

"That's right." The memory of Kimberly having her card declined gave her a jolt. Why would she tell her husband that someone had witnessed her embarrassment? Or had she neglected to tell Wayne that her card had been rejected? But Kimberly had seemed so angry at the time when she thought that Wayne might have missed paying the credit card bill. Lauren had told Zoe about the incident, her cousin declaring that she hoped something like that would never happen to her.

"What are you making? Kimberly's been telling me about this sweater she wants to knit."

"A scarf," Lauren answered.

"And I'm making a scarf, too." Zoe jumped into the conversation. "But I'm crocheting mine with multi-colored yarn."

"I don't know the difference between knitting and crocheting," Wayne admitted. "But hey, Kimberly offered you twenty percent off at the steakhouse, right? That's fine with me. When would you two like to come in again for dinner?"

"Oh – um – that's very kind of you," Lauren began awkwardly. "But—" she cast Zoe a *What do I say?!* glance.

"We're broke," Zoe told him cheerfully. "I had to wait until I had enough tip money before we could come here tonight. So it might be awhile before we can afford to visit the steakhouse again."

"You've read that crummy new review, haven't you?" Wayne's eyes flashed. "From the so-called food critic – Brandon somebody. Well, it's not true. That guy doesn't know what he's talking about. Todd, the *real* food critic, raved about my wagyu – and everything else I serve."

"I haven't read Brandon's review," Lauren said truthfully.

"You can read this one by Todd." He dug out his wallet from his back pocket and pulled out a folded sheet of paper. "See?" He thrust it in front of Lauren and unfolded it. His meaty finger stabbed at the text. "Todd says I serve amazing wagyu." His finger thudded on the table.

Lauren scanned the critique. It was dated last year and appeared to have been printed from a website – Todd's online column. The food critic seemed to have nothing but praise for Wayne's steakhouse.

"I can see that," Lauren told him.

"I read the review Brandon just gave you," Wayne informed them. "It seems he's more of a cupcake and pastry guy than a steak man. He wouldn't know good steak if it bit him on the butt!"

They were saved from answering by Cindy arriving with their dinner.

"Wayne, your order will be ready in a minute." She gestured to the take-out window near the kitchen door on the opposite side of the room.

"Thanks." He snatched up the review and stalked off.

"Wayne just said Brandon gave us a review – I wonder if he's updated it with Ed's pastries." Zoe pulled out her phone from her purse and looked at the screen.

"I hope so." Lauren's stomach fluttered.

Cindy set down a large white plate with a burger and a pile of golden, crispy French fries in front of each of them. The juicy-looking meat patty hung over the edge of the bun, and fronds of crisp lettuce and slices of fresh tomato peeked out. The aroma of smoky barbecue sauce teased Lauren's appetite and made her forget for a moment about their new review.

"Wow!" Zoe looked at her plate in admiration.

"Here's Annie's patty." Cindy gave Lauren a warm foil parcel.

"Thanks."

"Look!" Zoe held out her phone. "Brandon has updated our review – and it's all good!"

Lauren scanned the review, which praised Ed's pastries. She passed the phone to Cindy.

"That's great, guys." Cindy gave the phone back to Zoe. "But what was all that about with Wayne?" she asked.

"He got a bad review for the steakhouse," Lauren told her in a hushed voice.

"Oh – I heard about that when I clocked in this afternoon." Cindy shook her head. "It's a shame."

"Yes, it is." Zoe popped a fry into her mouth and chewed.

"The young guy who accompanied Todd was back here again," Cindy told them. "I hope he gives us a good review."

"Did you serve him?" Lauren asked curiously.

"Yes. And he was a total gentleman."

"That's good," Zoe replied.

"That's for sure. He was okay when he was with Todd the first time as well – when I told him Todd had left, he must have thought the bill had already been paid."

"Did you tell Brandon about that this time?" Zoe asked. "About how you had to pay for their order yourself?"

"No. I'm still embarrassed about the whole thing. Oh, I forgot to tell you! Gary covered the cost of their order, so it didn't come out of my paycheck after all. He said it was the least he could do after Todd's behavior."

"That's great." Zoe grinned.

"I'll leave you to enjoy your meal." Cindy beamed. "Give Annie a pat for me, won't you, Lauren?"

"Of course." Unable to resist temptation, Lauren picked up a golden French fry.

Once Cindy left, Zoe leaned forward. "I thought I'd better not say anything to Cindy about our steakhouse visit."

"Good thinking." Lauren chewed and swallowed, immediately wanting another delicious fry.

"I can't believe how upset Wayne got just now." Zoe shook her head. "I hope we never act like that if we ever get a bad review."

"Me too," Lauren replied. The image of Wayne's meaty finger stabbing the table in front of her flashed through her mind. She hoped she wouldn't lose her self-control like that – ever.

"It's sad that he carries that good review around with him," Zoe continued, lifting up the top of her burger bun to take a peek. "Do you think it's been in his wallet since Todd wrote the review? Or if he only put it in there since Brandon's bad review came out?"

"I don't know." Lauren crinkled her brow, trying to remember the way the print-out had looked. It hadn't seemed as if it had been folded and re-folded too many times. Perhaps Wayne *had* only placed it in his wallet recently.

The whoosh of the entrance door opening snagged Lauren's attention and she glanced around. Wayne stalked toward the door, carrying a take-out bag. His gaze flickered around the room, landing on Lauren's for a split-second, then he walked out onto the street.

CHAPTER 12

Lauren and Zoe enjoyed their burgers. They had such a good time that Lauren temporarily forgot about their interaction with Wayne that evening.

Once they returned home, Lauren fed Annie, the Norwegian Forest Cat brrting with pleasure at her supper.

"We'll definitely have to go back for more burgers soon." Zoe sipped a glass of water. "I'm going to have that smoky barbecue special again!"

"Me too."

"How about next week?" Zoe's eyes sparkled. "I should have enough in tips by then – hopefully. And we'll tell Gary not to take that burger off the menu – ever."

"Sounds like a plan." Lauren smiled. She'd enjoyed their meal tonight a lot more than their fancy steakhouse dinner. Perhaps she just wasn't a fine dining sort of girl.

Or maybe it was the fine dining food that had been the problem.

Lauren pushed that thought aside. She didn't want to think about bad reviews, the steakhouse, or Wayne's slightly scary attitude that evening. She just wanted to relax and enjoy the rest of the evening.

"Let's do some crochet!" Zoe headed toward the living room. "Or in your case, knitting!"

Lauren stifled a groan.

***

"Perhaps we should talk about suspects," Zoe said the next day. They were in the middle of opening up the café.

"Now?" Lauren looked at her cousin in surprise.

"Well, maybe not right this minute," Zoe replied. "But this case is going nowhere. Why haven't the police – or Mitch – made an arrest yet?"

"Maybe they have and they're keeping it hush-hush," Lauren suggested, wondering why she felt a need to defend Mitch.

"But why would that be?" Zoe pouted. "Besides, I don't think much stays secret in this town for long. Not everyone keeps their lips zipped."

"You've got a point." A smile edged Lauren's mouth.

"Annie, who do you think killed Todd? The food critic." Zoe turned to the feline, who sat up in her bed.

"Brrp?" Annie asked.

"Maybe we shouldn't ask her," Lauren said, remembering the effect finding Todd's body had seemed to have on the cat. "Maybe Annie doesn't like thinking about it."

"Sorry." Zoe looked contrite. "You're right. Forget I asked you that, Annie. You just have fun with your favorite customers today."

"Brrp." Annie settled down in her pink bed, looking as if she might have a little snooze before any customers arrived.

"We know it's not Brandon." Lauren unlocked the front door. "Not now we know why he didn't hear the killer when he was in the room next door."

"True." Zoe nodded, her brunette pixie bangs hitting her forehead. "And I like him."

"Me too," Lauren replied.

"So that leaves—" Zoe counted on her fingers as she headed behind the counter "—Claire, who worked with Todd years ago on the same newspaper, Cindy, Gary, Wayne, Kimberly—"

"But why would any of them murder him?" Lauren frowned. "Todd gave Wayne a good review last year."

"That's true." Zoe nodded.

"So if we're looking at people who had a problem with Todd, that leaves—"

"Gary and Cindy. Do you think it's strange she hasn't come into the café since the murder? And there are all the other people he's given a bad review to. Whoever they are," Zoe finished in a rush.

Lauren peered out of the front door. No customers. She didn't feel comfortable continuing the discussion if there were people around. Ed was already in the kitchen, concentrating on his pastry.

"I don't want it to be Cindy," Lauren said. "I like her."

"Me too. And I don't want it to be Gary. If he was in jail, who would make his burgers or think up new ones, like the smoky barbecue special we had last night?"

"His kitchen staff, I suppose," Lauren replied. "He probably has a trusted right-hand man he depends upon. But I don't want it to be Gary because I think he's a nice man—"

"Apart from when he got angry about Todd harassing Cindy," Zoe put in.

"True." Lauren nibbled her lip. "Do you know anyone who's received a bad review from Todd?" Lauren asked.

"I'll have to check. I can't remember reading one recently." Zoe pulled out her phone from her apron pocket. "I'm looking – and scrolling – and looking." Zoe pressed her phone screen. "I can't find anything right now."

"Hi, Hans." Lauren sent her cousin a warning look, then turned her attention back to the senior.

"Brrp." Annie scampered over to him.

"Hello, Lauren." The older man beamed. "And Annie. Where should I sit today, hmm, Liebchen?"

"Brrt," Annie said importantly, leading him to a small table near the counter. *Over here.*

***

Lauren, Zoe, and Annie were busy all day. A steady stream of customers came into the café, which was good for business, but left no time for Lauren and Zoe to talk about suspects.

At four o'clock, Lauren sent Annie home, accompanying her down the private hallway. "We'll close in an hour," she told the silver-gray tabby.

"Brrp," Annie replied, padding into the cottage. Lauren guessed when she and Zoe returned later, Annie would be curled up on the sofa, or perhaps playing with one of her toys.

"Phew!" Zoe flopped onto the stool behind the counter when Lauren returned to the cafe. "I can't believe how busy it's been for a Tuesday."

"You might have enough in tips for another smoky barbecue special." Lauren eyed the bursting to the brim tip jar. Silver coins glinted in the afternoon sun.

"You're right." Zoe perked up. "Awesome!"

"I think we've run out of cupcakes. And pastries." Lauren eyed the glass counter. Ed had baked some extra pastries when they'd realized today was going to be busy, but they'd sold out, along with her cupcakes.

"Mitch is out of luck if he comes in now," Zoe teased. She tapped her chin. "I haven't seen him the last few days – have you?"

"No." Lauren had wondered at his absence, then told herself not to be silly. He was a busy police detective. He probably didn't have time to come in for cupcakes and coffee, even if they were free right now, as a thank you for mowing her two lawns.

"I can't wait for five o'clock." Zoe stifled a yawn.

"I know what you mean." Lauren smiled at two departing customers who paid their bill.

"But there aren't any cupcakes to take home." Zoe pouted.

Lauren felt like pouting as well. A cupcake for dessert tonight would really hit the spot. They hadn't even had time for a proper lunchbreak.

"Maybe we should treat ourselves tonight." Zoe wiggled her feet. "What about pizza?"

"Good idea."

Zoe looked at the tip jar. "There should be plenty in there for my share."

"We'll order when we close up. We can have an early dinner."

"Now you're talking." Zoe grinned. "And hardly any dishes to take care of tonight!"

Their last customer left at five minutes to five.

Lauren and Zoe locked the entrance door right on the dot of five p.m. and quickly tidied up.

"I'll call for the pizza." Lauren picked up her phone.

"Pepperoni for me. Mmm." Zoe counted out some money from the tip jar and scrawled an IOU. "Here's my share." She pressed the dollar bills and coins into Lauren's hand.

"Thanks."

While Lauren put in the order, Zoe finished sweeping the floor.

Lauren ended the call. "It should be here in about twenty minutes."

"Awesome." Zoe grinned.

After they finished cleaning up, they headed to the cottage.

"We're home!" Zoe called out.

"Brrp?" Annie lay on her back in the kitchen, her front and back legs disemboweling a toy mouse.

"We're having pizza for dinner, Annie."

"Brrt!" Annie dropped the plaything and sat up.

"You know I don't think pizza is good for you," Lauren told the tabby.

"Brrp." Annie sounded sad as she looked appealingly at Lauren. She could have sworn the feline batted her eyelashes.

"Maybe you could have just a little of my Canadian bacon." Lauren gave in. Who wouldn't, looking at that sweet furry face? Surely just a tiny bit of cooked bacon would be okay for Annie?

Lauren, Zoe, and Annie relaxed while they waited for the pizza to arrive. Annie played with Lauren's red knitting wool and Zoe's multicolored crochet yarn, alternately batting each dangling fiber strand hanging down from the work in progress.

Ding dong.

"Pizza!" Zoe looked up from suspending the turquoise wool above Annie's paw.

"I'll go." Lauren grabbed the money from the kitchen table and headed toward the front door of the cottage.

Her stomach rumbled, and she opened the old wooden door with a smile on her face.

"Here you go – oh!" Her outstretched hand holding the money froze.

"Hello, Lauren." The man holding a large pizza box smiled at her.

"Wayne! What are you doing here?" Lauren frowned.

"I was getting pizza for myself before I started work tonight. You know when you have a craving that just won't go away? So I called my sous chef and told him I'd be a little late."

"Zoe and I were craving pizza tonight, too," Lauren told him, still bemused as to why he stood there on her doorstep with the pizza they'd ordered.

"While I was in the shop, the driver had just called in sick, so I volunteered to drop off your pizza. Otherwise, the owner would have had to leave his teenage nephew in charge, who hasn't been working there long."

"Thank you." Lauren handed him the money. "That's very kind of you."

"You're welcome." Wayne handed her the hot, fragrant box. "Half pepperoni, half Canadian bacon and mushroom, right?"

"Right."

"I paid for your order myself, so I don't have to stop back at the pizza place on the way to the steakhouse."

"Thanks," Lauren said again. "Zoe's starving, so I'd better get this inside."

"Sure." He nodded, then turned to go. "Oh, by the way." He swung around to face her. "Don't forget to come by the steakhouse with Zoe when you get a chance. Twenty percent off and I'll throw in a nice piece of steak for you to take home for Annie."

Lauren wasn't sure what to say. "I'll make sure to mention it to Zoe – and Annie."

"You do that. My steak is the best. Todd said so."

"Right." Lauren nodded, just wanting to take the pizza inside and shut the door, but she didn't want to be rude, either.

"Hey, did you see that Gary got a new review by that Brandon guy?"

"He did?" Lauren stared at Wayne. "When was that?"

"This afternoon. I was reading some news articles on that site and a pop-up appeared saying that Brandon had posted a new review. So I clicked on it to see what it was about."

"What did the review say?" Lauren asked. She'd have to tell Zoe about it.

"He got a good one." Wayne's mouth twisted. "So Gary must have done something right. Yeah, his burgers are good, but it's not quite the same as having an Ang – wagyu steak."

Was Wayne about to say Angus – as in Angus steak?

Lauren's eyes widened as a snippet of conversation flashed through her brain – Brandon telling them that Wayne's wagyu steak reminded him of Angus. Lauren knew that Angus, although good quality, was a far cheaper variety of meat than wagyu.

Surely Wayne hadn't—

"You know, don't you?" Wayne snarled. He pushed her into the cottage, the corner of the hot pizza box hitting Lauren's stomach.

"Know what?" Lauren attempted to bluff as Wayne marched her down the hall and into the living room.

"I substituted Angus steak for pricey wagyu steak."

"You didn't!" Zoe jumped up from the sofa and stared at him.

"Brrt?" Annie looked from Lauren to Wayne, concern on her furry face.

"It's okay, Annie." Lauren tried to speak soothingly. "Why don't you go to my bedroom for a bit?" She didn't want Wayne to hurt her.

Annie first looked at Lauren, and then at Zoe. "Brrp." *No.*

"Annie's not the problem here." Wayne pushed Lauren forward. She stumbled.

"Brandon didn't think you served wagyu," Zoe told him. "Now it makes sense why I didn't think your wagyu should have been so expensive. I couldn't taste much difference between it and ordinary steak." She turned to Lauren. "I'm sorry I made us try it."

"It's okay," Lauren said, still holding the pizza box. The savory aromas of pepperoni, Canadian bacon, and mushroom now made her stomach churn. She was about to place it on the coffee table, then had second thoughts. It might come in handy as a weapon.

"Yeah." Wayne grimaced. "I had a good thing going with Todd, and then he had to spoil it. When he reviewed my steakhouse last year, he knew right away that my "wagyu" wasn't wagyu at all. But it didn't bother him. He came to the kitchen afterward and requested to talk privately. So we went outside. He told me if I paid him five hundred dollars per month, he'd keep my secret – that I was serving up Angus beef and calling it wagyu. He'd also throw in a glowing review which would increase my customer base."

"He didn't!" Zoe's mouth parted. "Brandon said he was a stickler for good food and—"

"It was an act," Wayne informed her. "According to Todd, Brandon didn't have a clue about his side business. Todd was just out for what he could get."

"Like you?" Lauren asked, her heart hammering.

"I didn't start out trying to deceive people." Wayne's shoulders slumped for a second. "It's my wife Kimberly. She's got a shopping addiction. She just won't stop spending money. I already took out a second mortgage on the house. Her spending is the reason I started the wagyu scam in the first place."

"What gave you the idea?" Zoe asked.

"I watched a show about wagyu on TV. It said how much places charge for a genuine steak. I'd just received the latest credit card bill – over the limit again – and I was desperate. I was already having problems making the payments on the second mortgage as well as paying the minimum off the credit card every month." He shook his head. "As soon as I pay the monthly bill, Kimberly spends up again."

"I'm sorry," Lauren replied. She was. But she also didn't want Wayne to feel so desperate that he thought he had no choice but to hurt them.

"What about marriage counselling?" Zoe asked.

"We saw someone." He snorted. "Kimberly promised she'd try not to spend so much, but after a few weeks she said it was just too hard and didn't she deserve nice things? Of course she does. She's my wife, and I love her. And then we got the bill for the counselling and, well …"

"So what happened after Todd wrote you that good review?" Lauren asked, wondering if she was doing the right thing in keeping him talking.

"Business was great." A brief smile. "I was able to pay down the credit card – some of the balance, anyway. Then Todd contacted me and said the price had gone up. I now had to pay him one thousand dollars per month."

"No!" Zoe blinked.

"And then, every couple of months after that, Todd would call me and up the price again. When he came to town a couple of weeks ago, he increased the price to two thousand." Wayne shook his head. "It was too much."

"What happened?" Lauren asked.

"Brrp?" Annie seemed to ask as well.

"I went over to his motel room to talk to him, asking him to be reasonable. I'm not getting as many customers now. Not like when his review first appeared in his column."

"That's because they're not impressed with the 'wagyu'," Zoe said. "Like we weren't."

Wayne glared at her.

"Oops." Zoe mimed zipping her lips shut.

"He said because I told him he was getting greedy, forget about paying him two thousand. It was now going to be three thousand. And if I didn't give him the money, he would report me to the police for fraud. I didn't have a choice." Wayne looked pleadingly at them, as if expecting them to understand his position.

"If you explain it to the authorities, and tell them the financial stress you were under, maybe they'll understand," Lauren said.

"I can't." Wayne's face twisted. "What will Kimberly do if I'm in prison?"

"Get a job?" Zoe suggested.

"She doesn't have any skills. She's been a housewife for the last twenty years. She can't even balance her checkbook. That's one of the reasons we're in a hole financially."

"Maybe she could be a personal shopper," Zoe said in a helpful tone. "She'll get her shopping fix but she'll be spending other people's money."

"*Graah!* Why didn't I think of that?" Anger flashed across his face. "I mightn't have needed to kill Todd after all!"

"There's still time to turn yourself in," Lauren urged. "Zoe and I will tell the police that you didn't hurt us."

"It's too late." Wayne clenched his fists. "Too late to do anything! Except make sure nobody knows it was me!"

He lunged toward Lauren.

She shrieked and opened the pizza box. As he loomed over her, she smashed the pizza in his face.

"Ow!" he screamed, clawing at his face. "Hot!"

"Run!" Before Lauren could pick up Annie, the feline pushed the pizza box a couple of inches in front of Wayne's large feet. He stumbled over the cardboard, falling to his knees, the melted cheese and sauce from the pizza obscuring his vision.

"Quick!" Zoe vibrated with urgency as Lauren snatched up Annie.

They ran out of the cottage.

"Lauren?" Mitch's vehicle was parked outside her gate. He looked at her in concern, then sprang into action, his hand going to his hip holster. He strode toward her front door.

"It's Wayne," Lauren gasped, Annie held securely in her arms. "He killed Todd."

"And he's got hot pizza on his face," Zoe told him.

"Stay there," he ordered.

They watched him enter the cottage.

"I wonder why Mitch is here." Zoe crinkled her brow.

"I'm just glad he is." Lauren pressed a kiss on Annie's forehead. "Aren't you?" she asked her.

"Brrt." *Yes.*

Lauren and Zoe stepped onto the sidewalk and stood right next to Mitch's car.

"In case we need to make a quick getaway," Zoe said, trying to make a joke of the situation.

"Brrt!"

EPILOGUE

Mitch marched a handcuffed Wayne out of Lauren's cottage. His face was red and blotchy. Pieces of pepperoni and bacon stuck to his cheeks and chin.

"I've called for backup," Mitch told them. "I'll wait until they get here." He helped Wayne into the car and locked the doors. "Tell me what happened."

They did, Annie wide-eyed during the conversation. She kept sneaking glances between Lauren and Mitch while she nestled in Lauren's arms.

"And then Annie pushed the pizza box toward Wayne so he would fall over it." Zoe giggled. Lauren thought it might be from reaction. "And he did!"

"That's one clever cat." Mitch sounded sincere.

"Brrt!"

Once assistance arrived, Mitch departed with Wayne, while a

uniformed officer took Lauren and Zoe's statements.

When he left, Zoe locked the cottage door behind him.

"Phew!" She flopped onto the living room sofa. "I'm bushed." She checked her watch. "I can't believe it's not even eight p.m.!"

"I know." Lauren nodded. She'd just given Annie something to eat and now she held paper towels in her hands. "What are we going to do about this mess?" She looked in dismay at the oyster hued carpet, a large section covered in red sauce, mozzarella cheese, and the pizza toppings.

"I'll help." Zoe sighed and kneeled on the carpet.

"I hope Wayne's face didn't get burned." Lauren swiped at the carpet with the paper cloth.

"If he did, it was his own fault." Zoe stabbed at a cheesy stain. "He shouldn't have threatened us like that."

"Brrt!" Annie trotted in from the kitchen and seemed to agree. "Brrt!"

"You were a big help, Annie," Lauren told her. "If Wayne hadn't lost his balance tripping over the pizza box—"

"Don't." Zoe shuddered. She reached for the cat and gave her a gentle stroke. "We all played a part in saving the three of us – well, you and Annie did." She looked downhearted. "I didn't get to do anything."

"You made sure we were all together when we ran out of the house," Lauren told her.

"Brrt!" *Yes.*

"That's what family is for," Zoe replied, her expression cheering slightly.

"Brrt!"

***

Lauren didn't discover why Mitch had arrived at her cottage that evening. He stopped by the café the

237

next day to inform her that Wayne was pleading guilty to the murder of Todd Fane.

"Good," Zoe replied.

"What will happen to Kimberly?" Lauren asked.

"Wayne swears that she didn't know anything about substituting Angus steak for wagyu, or that Todd was blackmailing him," Mitch answered. "It looks like she'll either have to run the steakhouse herself or sell it."

"Poor Kimberly," Lauren said.

"She could always ask Gary for advice," Zoe mused. "I know he specializes in burgers, but food is food. Or she could always ask us for help – like with desserts."

"Good thinking," Lauren replied.

"I'm talking to her again this afternoon, so I'll pass on your suggestions."

"Brrt!" *Good idea.*

"Can I make you a latte?" Lauren said, her hands poised at the espresso machine.

"That would be great." His lips tilted upward in a smile.

"I'll just see if Ed needs me in the kitchen." Zoe faded away with a stifled giggle.

Lauren forgot what she was about to do – she was too busy gazing into Mitch's dark brown eyes. And he seemed to be gazing back at her.

After a few seconds, Annie enquired: "Brrt?"

Lauren blinked, the spell broken. Latte. Right. The machine growled as the ground beans filled the portafilter, the scents of dark cherry and chocolate permeating the air.

"Have you got any vanilla cupcakes?" Mitch asked.

She peeked at the glass case. "Just one."

"Just one is all I need." His gaze locked with hers once more.

"Brrt?"

Mitch cleared his throat. Hesitated. "Would you like to go out with me sometime, Lauren?"

"Yes."

"Brrt!"

THE END

AUTHOR NOTE and TITLES BY JINTY JAMES

Annie is based on my own Norwegian Forest Cat, who was also called Annie.

I hope you enjoyed reading this mystery. Sign up to my newsletter at www.JintyJames.com and be among the first to discover when my next book is published!

Have you read:

Purrs and Peril – A Norwegian Forest Cat Café Cozy Mystery – Book 1

Maddie Goodwell Series (fun witch cozies)

Spells and Spiced Latte - A Coffee Witch Cozy Mystery - Maddie Goodwell 1

Visions and Vanilla Cappuccino - A Coffee Witch Cozy Mystery - Maddie Goodwell 2

Magic and Mocha – A Coffee Witch Cozy Mystery – Maddie Goodwell 3

Enchantments and Espresso – A Coffee Witch Cozy Mystery – Maddie Goodwell 4

Familiars and French Roast - A Coffee Witch Cozy Mystery – Maddie Goodwell 5

Incantations and Iced Coffee – A Coffee Witch Cozy Mystery – Maddie Goodwell 6

Made in the USA
Columbia, SC
03 September 2020